The Divine Heart

Christian romance fiction, Volume 1

Michelle Renee Thomas

Published by FaithLight Publishers, 2024.

This is a work of fiction. Similarities to real people, places, or events are entirely coincidental.

THE DIVINE HEART

First edition. November 19, 2024.

Copyright © 2024 Michelle Renee Thomas.

ISBN: 979-8230228004

Written by Michelle Renee Thomas.

Table of Contents

The Divine Heart (Christian romance fiction, #1) 1
Chapter 2: The Heart of Sacrifice 6
Chapter 3: Love in the Face of Trials 13
Chapter 4: Forgiveness as an Act of Love 20
Chapter 5: Patience and Long-Suffering 28
Chapter 6: The Covenant of Marriage 36
Chapter 7: The Role of Prayer in Love 44
Chapter 8: The Healing Power of Love 54
Chapter 10: The Joy of Love 71
Chapter 11: Overcoming Fear with Love 81
Chapter 12: Love as a Reflection of Faith 91
Chapter 13: The Eternal Nature of Love 101
Chapter 14: Love as a Witness 112
Chapter 15: The Divine Heart of Love 121

To those who seek to know the depths of God's love and to reflect it in their lives,

This book is dedicated to you.

May the divine heart of love that flows from our Creator inspire you to love selflessly, forgive endlessly, and live with a heart full of grace.

And to my family and friends, whose love and support have been a living testament to the truths within these pages—thank you for being a constant reminder of God's enduring love.

Introduction

In a world that often defines love in transient, superficial terms, the Christian understanding of love stands as a beacon of hope, grounded in something far greater than human emotion or desire. At the heart of this understanding is the belief that God is the ultimate source of love. This chapter will explore this profound truth, as rooted in the Scriptures, particularly in 1 John 4:7-8, where the Apostle John declares, "Beloved, let us love one another, for love is from God, and whoever loves has been born of God and knows God. Anyone who does not love does not know God, because God is love."

The Nature of Divine Love

The concept of love is one that transcends cultures, religions, and philosophies. It is a universal language that everyone understands, yet it is often misunderstood, misrepresented, and misapplied. Human love, while beautiful, is often conditional, limited, and flawed. It is influenced by personal desires, expectations, and emotions. In contrast, the love of God—often referred to as "agape" love in Christian theology—is unconditional, limitless, and perfect. It is a love that is not based on what we do but on who God is.

God's love is described in the Bible as eternal (Jeremiah 31:3), unchanging (James 1:17), and sacrificial (John 3:16). It is a love that seeks the well-being of others without expecting anything in return. This is the kind of love that God has for humanity, a love that was ultimately demonstrated through the life, death, and resurrection of Jesus Christ.

In 1 John 4:7-8, John emphasizes that love is not merely an attribute of God but is the very essence of His being. To say "God is love" means that love is not just something God does, but it is who He is. His actions are always motivated by love because love is the core of His character. This is a radical and transformative understanding of love that has profound implications for how we view God and how we relate to one another.

The Foundation of All Relationships

If God is the source of love, then it follows that all true love in human relationships must be rooted in Him. This is a foundational truth for Christian living. Whether it is the love between husband and wife, parent and child, or friends and neighbors, the love that we share with others is a reflection of God's love for us.

This means that our ability to love others is directly connected to our relationship with God. The more we know God, the more we understand His love for us, and the more we are able to love others with that same kind of love. This is why John says that whoever loves has been born of God and knows God. Love is the evidence of a relationship with God. It is the fruit of the Spirit working in our lives.

Conversely, if we do not love, it reveals a lack of connection with God. John is clear: "Anyone who does not love does not know God." This is a sobering statement, reminding us that our love for others is not optional; it is essential. It is the proof that we know God and that His love is at work in us.

God's Love Manifested in Christ

The ultimate manifestation of God's love is found in the person of Jesus Christ. The Bible tells us that "God so loved the world, that he gave his only Son, that whoever believes in him should not perish but have eternal life" (John 3:16). This verse, perhaps the most well-known in all of Scripture, encapsulates the heart of the Gospel—the good news of God's love for humanity.

God's love is not abstract or theoretical; it is concrete and active. It is a love that moves toward us, even when we are far from Him. Romans 5:8 says, "But God shows his love for us in that while we were still sinners, Christ died for us." This is the essence of agape love: it is self-giving, sacrificial, and unconditional.

In Jesus, we see the fullness of God's love. He is the embodiment of love in action. He healed the sick, fed the hungry, and welcomed the outcast. He forgave sins, offered grace, and extended mercy. And ultimately, He laid down His life for us, the greatest act of love the world has ever known.

This love is the model for our love. Jesus Himself said, "A new commandment I give to you, that you love one another: just as I have loved you, you also are to love one another" (John 13:34). The standard of love that we are called to is nothing less than the love of Christ. This is not something we can achieve on our own; it is only possible through the power of the Holy Spirit working in us.

Love as the Mark of Discipleship

The early Christians understood that love was to be the defining mark of their community. In a world where divisions and hostility were common, the love that Christians had for one another set them apart. Jesus said, "By this all people will know that you are my disciples, if you have love for one another" (John 13:35).

This love was not just an inward-looking, exclusive love for those within the community. It was a love that extended to the stranger, the enemy, and the marginalized. It was a love that crossed social, ethnic, and religious boundaries. The early church was a radical community of love, and it was this love that drew people to the message of the Gospel.

The Apostle Paul echoed this when he wrote to the Corinthians, "If I speak in the tongues of men and of angels, but have not love, I am a noisy gong or a clanging cymbal. And if I have prophetic powers, and understand all mysteries and all knowledge, and if I have all faith, so as to remove mountains, but have not love, I am nothing" (1 Corinthians 13:1-2). For Paul, love was the essential quality that gave meaning to all other spiritual gifts and actions. Without love, all else is empty and meaningless.

This is a powerful reminder for us today. In a world that often values power, success, and achievement, the Christian is called to value love above all. It is love that gives purpose to our lives and to our relationships. It is love that reflects the heart of God to the world.

The Transformative Power of Love

One of the most remarkable aspects of God's love is its transformative power. When we encounter the love of God, it changes us. It softens our hearts, renews our minds, and compels us to live differently. This is why Paul prays for the Ephesians, "that Christ may dwell in your hearts through faith—that you, being rooted and grounded in love, may have strength to comprehend with all the saints what is the breadth and length and height and depth, and to know the love of Christ that surpasses knowledge, that you may be filled with all the fullness of God" (Ephesians 3:17-19).

To be "rooted and grounded in love" means that love is the foundation of our lives. It is the soil in which our faith grows. When we are secure in God's love for us, we are free to love others without fear or insecurity. We no longer need to protect ourselves or hold back; we can give ourselves fully in love, just as Christ gave Himself for us.

This kind of love has the power to transform relationships. It heals wounds, restores trust, and builds unity. It creates communities where people are valued, respected, and cared for. It draws people to the light of Christ, where they can experience the love of God for themselves.

The love of God also transforms how we see ourselves. In a world that often tells us we are not enough, God's love affirms our worth and value. We are loved, not because of what we do, but because of who we are—God's beloved children. This gives us a deep sense of security and identity, freeing us from the need to seek approval or validation from others.

Living in the Light of God's Love

As Christians, we are called to live in the light of God's love. This means allowing His love to shape every aspect of our lives—our thoughts, our actions, our relationships, and our decisions. It means continually returning to the source of love, spending time in God's presence, and allowing His love to fill and overflow in us.

This is not always easy. We live in a world that often promotes selfishness, pride, and division. But as we keep our eyes on Christ, we are reminded that love is the most excellent way (1 Corinthians 12:31). It is the path that leads to true life, both now and in eternity.

One of the ways we can cultivate a life rooted in love is through prayer. Prayer is the place where we connect with God and receive His love. It is where we bring our struggles, our fears, and our failures, and where we are reminded of God's grace and mercy. In prayer, we are filled with the Holy Spirit, who empowers us to love others as Christ has loved us.

Another way to live in the light of God's love is through community. God did not create us to walk this journey alone. We need one another to encourage, support, and challenge us to grow in love. The church is meant to be a community of love, where we practice loving one another and where we learn to extend that love to the world.

Finally, we live in the light of God's love by serving others. Love is not just a feeling; it is an action. It is something we do. Jesus said,

"Greater love has no one than this, that someone lay down his life for his friends" (John 15:13). We may not be called to physically lay down our lives, but we are called to lay down our pride, our comfort, and our time for the sake of others. In serving others, we reflect the love of Christ and make His love known to the world.

Conclusion

The source of true love is not found in human effort or emotion but in God Himself. He is the fountain from which all love flows. As we come to know God and experience His love for us, we are transformed. This love becomes the foundation of our lives, shaping our relationships, our actions, and our purpose.

In a world that often misunderstands and misrepresents love, we are called to be a people who reflect the true love of God. This is not something we can do on our own; it is the work of the Holy Spirit in us. But as we remain rooted and grounded in God's love, we will be empowered to love others as Christ has loved us.

May we, like the Apostle John, be people who know and experience the love of God, and who share that love with a world in desperate need of it. For in this, we fulfill the greatest commandment: "You shall love the Lord your God with all your heart and with all your soul and with all your mind. This is the great and first commandment. And a second is like it: You shall love your neighbor as yourself. On these two commandments depend all the Law and the Prophets" (Matthew 22:37-40).

The divine heart of love is a heart that beats for us, a heart that never gives up, and a heart that continually draws us closer to the One who is Love Himself. As we journey through life, may we always return to this source, allowing the love of God to fill us, change us, and flow through us to a world that so desperately needs it.

Chapter 2: The Heart of Sacrifice

Introduction

Love, as the world often portrays it, is a complex and multifaceted emotion. It is depicted in grand gestures, romantic entanglements, and profound connections between individuals. Yet, in the Christian understanding, love transcends mere emotion or affection. It is deeply rooted in sacrifice—a theme central to the Gospel and the life of Jesus Christ. In John 15:13, Jesus declares, "Greater love has no one than this, that someone lay down his life for his friends." This verse not only encapsulates the essence of Christ's mission but also sets the standard for what true love entails. It challenges us to reconsider our understanding of love and to recognize that, at its core, love is sacrificial.

In this chapter, we will explore the sacrificial nature of Christ's love and how it serves as the ultimate example for us to follow. We will delve into the theological significance of sacrifice in the Christian faith, examine the implications of living a life marked by sacrificial love, and consider the transformative power that such love can have in our relationships and communities.

The Sacrificial Love of Christ

To understand the heart of sacrifice, we must first look to the life and ministry of Jesus Christ. From the moment of His incarnation, Christ's entire life was marked by sacrifice. The Apostle Paul, in his letter to the Philippians, writes, "Though he was in the form of God, [Jesus] did not count equality with God a thing to be grasped, but emptied himself, by taking the form of a servant, being born in the likeness of men" (Philippians 2:6-7). This "emptying" or "kenosis," as theologians often refer to it, signifies Christ's willingness to relinquish His divine privileges and enter into the human condition.

Jesus' sacrifice did not begin at the cross; it began with His incarnation. The very act of God becoming man is a profound act of love and humility. In taking on human flesh, Jesus subjected Himself to the limitations, sufferings, and temptations that come with being human. Yet, He did so out of love—for the purpose of redeeming humanity from sin and restoring us to a right relationship with God.

As Jesus walked the earth, His life was characterized by acts of selflessness and service. He healed the sick, fed the hungry, and preached the good news to the poor. He associated with sinners, tax collectors, and outcasts—those whom society had rejected. In doing so, Jesus demonstrated that true love is not about seeking one's own benefit but about giving oneself for the sake of others. His love was not selective or conditional; it was universal and unconditional.

The ultimate expression of Christ's sacrificial love, however, is found in His willingness to lay down His life on the cross. The cross stands at the center of Christian faith as the supreme act of love and sacrifice. Jesus, the sinless Son of God, willingly took upon Himself the sins of the world and endured the punishment that we deserved. As Isaiah prophesied, "He was wounded for our transgressions; he was crushed for our iniquities; upon him was the chastisement that brought us peace, and with his stripes we are healed" (Isaiah 53:5).

This act of sacrifice was not merely a tragic event in history; it was a deliberate, purposeful act of redemption. Jesus Himself declared, "The Son of Man came not to be served but to serve, and to give his life as a ransom for many" (Matthew 20:28). In His sacrifice, Jesus not only paid the price for our sins but also revealed the depth of God's love for humanity. As Paul writes in Romans 5:8, "God shows his love for us in that while we were still sinners, Christ died for us."

The Theological Significance of Sacrifice

The concept of sacrifice is deeply ingrained in the biblical narrative, from the Old Testament to the New. In the Old Testament, sacrifices were a central part of Israel's worship and relationship with God. The sacrificial system, established in the Law of Moses, involved the offering of animals, grains, and other substances as a means of atoning for sin and expressing devotion to God. These sacrifices were symbolic acts, pointing to the need for purification, forgiveness, and reconciliation with God.

However, the sacrifices of the Old Testament were ultimately insufficient to deal with the root problem of sin. The writer of Hebrews makes this clear:

"For it is impossible for the blood of bulls and goats to take away sins" (Hebrews 10:4). These sacrifices were temporary, needing to be repeated year after year. They served as a foreshadowing of the perfect and final sacrifice that would be made by Jesus Christ.

In the New Testament, Jesus is described as the "Lamb of God, who takes away the sin of the world" (John 1:29). He is the fulfillment of the sacrificial system—a sacrifice that is perfect, sufficient, and eternal. Unlike the sacrifices of the Old Testament, which had to be offered repeatedly, Jesus' sacrifice was once and for all. The author of Hebrews emphasizes this point: "But when Christ had offered for all time a single sacrifice for sins, he sat down at the right hand of God" (Hebrews 10:12).

Theologically, the sacrifice of Christ accomplishes several key things. First, it atones for sin. Sin, which separates humanity from God, requires justice—a penalty must be paid. In His sacrifice, Jesus took upon Himself the penalty for our sins, satisfying the demands of justice and making it possible for us to be forgiven and reconciled to God.

Second, the sacrifice of Christ demonstrates the love and mercy of God. It shows that God was willing to go to the greatest lengths to restore us to Himself, even to the point of sacrificing His own Son. This is the ultimate expression of divine love—a love that is self-giving, sacrificial, and redemptive.

Third, the sacrifice of Christ is the foundation for the new covenant between God and humanity. In the Old Testament, the covenant between God and Israel was based on the Law, with sacrifices serving as a means of maintaining the relationship. In the New Testament, the new covenant is based on the blood of Christ, which secures our forgiveness and brings us into a new, everlasting relationship with God. As Jesus said at the Last Supper, "This cup that is poured out for you is the new covenant in my blood" (Luke 22:20).

The Call to Sacrificial Love

If the sacrifice of Christ is the ultimate expression of love, then as His followers, we are called to embody that same sacrificial love in our own lives. This is not merely an abstract ideal; it is a practical and demanding call to action. Jesus Himself made this clear when He said, "If anyone would come after me, let him deny himself and take up his cross daily and follow me" (Luke 9:23).

Taking up our cross means embracing a life of self-denial, service, and sacrifice. It means putting the needs of others before our own, seeking the well-being of others even at personal cost, and living in a way that reflects the sacrificial love of Christ. This is the essence of discipleship—a life marked by love, not just in word but in deed.

The Apostle Paul, in his letter to the Romans, urges believers to "present your bodies as a living sacrifice, holy and acceptable to God, which is your spiritual worship" (Romans 12:1). This idea of being a "living sacrifice" speaks to the ongoing nature of sacrificial love. It is not a one-time act but a continuous way of life. It involves every aspect of our being—our thoughts, our actions, our relationships, and our decisions. It is a daily offering of ourselves to God and to others.

Paul also provides practical examples of what this sacrificial love looks like in action. In Philippians 2:3-4, he writes, "Do nothing from selfish ambition or conceit, but in humility count others more significant than yourselves. Let each of you look not only to his own interests but also to the interests of others." Here, Paul emphasizes the importance of humility and selflessness in our relationships with others. Sacrificial love requires that we put aside our own desires, ambitions, and pride, and instead seek the good of others.

In his letter to the Ephesians, Paul further elaborates on this concept of sacrificial love, specifically in the context of marriage. He writes, "Husbands, love your wives, as Christ loved the church and gave himself up for her" (Ephesians 5:25). This verse is often cited in discussions of Christian marriage, but its implications go far beyond the marital relationship. It sets a standard for all relationships, calling us to love others in the same way that Christ loved the church—selflessly, sacrificially, and unconditionally.

The Transformative Power of Sacrificial Love

Sacrificial love is not only a reflection of Christ's love for us; it is also a powerful force for transformation. When we live lives marked by sacrificial love, we participate in God's redemptive work in the world. We become instruments of His grace, agents of His peace, and witnesses to His love.

One of the most significant ways that sacrificial love transforms us is by freeing us from the bondage of selfishness. Selfishness is the root of much of the brokenness and suffering in the world. It leads to greed, envy, strife, and division. When we focus solely on ourselves—our needs, our desires, our ambitions—we become isolated and disconnected from others. Sacrificial love, on the other hand, draws us out of ourselves and into relationship with others. It helps us to see the world through the eyes of Christ, with compassion, empathy, and concern for the well-being of others.

Moreover, sacrificial love has the power to heal and restore relationships. In a world where relationships are often strained by misunderstandings, conflicts, and hurts, the willingness to sacrifice for the sake of others can bring about reconciliation and renewal. When we choose to forgive, to serve, and to put others before ourselves, we create an environment where love can flourish and where broken relationships can be mended.

The impact of sacrificial love is not limited to personal relationships; it extends to the broader community and society. Throughout history, individuals and movements motivated by sacrificial love have brought about profound social change. From the early Christians who cared for the sick and the poor, to modern-day examples of those who work for justice, peace, and the dignity of all people, sacrificial love has been a driving force for good in the world.

Consider the life of Mother Teresa, who devoted herself to serving the poorest of the poor in the slums of Calcutta. Her life was a living testament to the power of sacrificial love. She once said, "Love, to be real, must cost—it must hurt—it must empty us of self." Her ministry, which began with a simple act of compassion, grew into a global movement that continues to touch the lives of countless people. Mother Teresa's example shows us that sacrificial love, even in small acts, has the power to transform lives and communities.

Challenges to Sacrificial Love

While the call to sacrificial love is clear in Scripture, it is not without its challenges. In a culture that often values self-interest, comfort, and convenience, the idea of living a life marked by sacrifice can seem daunting, if not impossible. We may fear that if we give too much of ourselves, we will be left with nothing. We may worry that others will take advantage of our generosity, or that our efforts will go unappreciated or unnoticed.

These are valid concerns, and they reflect the reality that sacrificial love often involves risk and vulnerability. When we choose to love sacrificially, we open ourselves up to the possibility of rejection, disappointment, and pain. However, it is precisely in these moments of vulnerability that the true nature of love is revealed. As C.S. Lewis once wrote, "To love at all is to be vulnerable. Love anything, and your heart will be wrung and possibly broken. If you want to make sure of keeping it intact, you must give it to no one, not even an animal."

Sacrificial love requires trust—trust in God, that He will provide for our needs, and trust in others, that they will receive and respond to our love. It also requires perseverance. There will be times when our efforts to love others seem fruitless, when our sacrifices go unnoticed or unappreciated. In these moments, we must remember that our call to love is not contingent on the response of others. We are called to love because Christ first loved us, and it is His love that sustains and empowers us.

Practical Ways to Live Out Sacrificial Love

Living a life of sacrificial love begins with small, everyday actions. It does not necessarily require grand gestures or heroic deeds; rather, it is about being faithful in the ordinary moments of life. Here are some practical ways to cultivate sacrificial love in our daily lives:

1. Prioritize Others: Make a conscious effort to put the needs and interests of others before your own. This could mean offering your time, resources, or attention to someone who needs it, even when it is inconvenient.

2. Practice Forgiveness: Forgiveness is one of the most challenging yet essential aspects of sacrificial love. Let go of grudges and choose to forgive those who have wronged you, even when it is difficult.

3. Serve Your Community: Look for opportunities to serve those around you, whether through volunteering, acts of kindness, or simply being present for someone in need. Service is a tangible expression of sacrificial love.

4. Cultivate Humility: Recognize that sacrificial love requires humility. Be willing to admit when you are wrong, to apologize, and to seek reconciliation in your relationships.

5. Pray for Others: Lift up others in prayer, asking God to bless them, guide them, and meet their needs. Prayer is a powerful way to express love for others, even when you cannot be physically present.

6. Be Generous: Whether it is with your time, money, or talents, practice generosity. Give freely, without expecting anything in return.

7. Listen and Empathize: Take the time to listen to others, to understand their struggles, and to offer support and encouragement. Listening is a simple yet profound way to show love.

8. Be Patient: Love is patient. Practice patience in your interactions with others, especially in difficult or frustrating situations.

9. Encourage and Uplift: Use your words to build others up, to affirm their worth, and to encourage them in their walk with God. Words have the power to heal and inspire.

10. Live with Integrity: Let your actions align with your values and beliefs. Living with integrity is a way of honoring God and loving others through your example.

Conclusion

The heart of sacrifice is the heart of love—a love that is willing to give of itself for the sake of others. This is the love that Jesus Christ exemplified in His life, death, and resurrection, and it is the love to which we are called as His followers.

In a world that often prioritizes self-interest and convenience, sacrificial love stands as a powerful witness to the transforming power of the Gospel. It challenges us to step outside of ourselves, to embrace vulnerability, and to live lives marked by selflessness and service. While it is not always easy, sacrificial love is deeply rewarding. It brings us closer to the heart of God, strengthens our relationships, and has the power to change the world.

As we seek to live out this call to sacrificial love, may we be inspired by the example of Christ and empowered by the Holy Spirit. May we remember that true love is not about what we can gain, but about what we are willing to give. And in giving, may we discover the fullness of life that comes from living in the heart of sacrifice—the heart of Christ Himself.

Chapter 3: Love in the Face of Trials

Introduction

Love is often depicted as an emotion of joy, peace, and fulfillment. It is the bond that connects us to others, bringing warmth and comfort to our hearts. However, love is also tested, and its strength is most evident not during moments of ease, but in the midst of trials and tribulations. The Apostle James, in his epistle, writes, "Blessed is the man who remains steadfast under trial, for when he has stood the test he will receive the crown of life, which God has promised to those who love him" (James 1:12). This verse not only speaks to the endurance of faith but also highlights the resilience of love when it is confronted with challenges.

In this chapter, we will explore the relationship between love and trials, delving into how love is both tested and strengthened in the face of adversity. We will reflect on the theological implications of trials in the Christian life, examine how love can endure and grow through difficulties, and consider practical ways to cultivate a love that perseveres even in the most challenging circumstances.

The Nature of Trials

Trials are an inevitable part of the human experience. They come in various forms—physical illness, financial hardship, relational conflicts, loss, and persecution, to name a few. For the Christian, trials are not just random occurrences but are seen as opportunities for spiritual growth and maturation. James begins his epistle by encouraging believers to "count it all joy" when they meet trials of various kinds (James 1:2). This counterintuitive command suggests that trials, while painful and challenging, serve a greater purpose in the life of a believer.

In the context of love, trials can be particularly challenging. Love, by its very nature, involves vulnerability and sacrifice. When love is tested, it is easy to succumb to fear, doubt, and self-preservation. Yet, it is precisely in these moments that love has the potential to shine the brightest. The testing of love reveals its authenticity and depth, just as the testing of faith reveals the genuineness of one's trust in God.

The Testing of Love

The testing of love occurs in various ways. It may be tested by external circumstances—such as illness, financial stress, or the actions of others—or by internal struggles, such as doubt, fear, or insecurity. Regardless of the source, the testing of love challenges us to remain steadfast in our commitment to others, even when it is difficult or painful.

One of the most profound examples of love being tested is found in the story of Job. Job was a man who loved God and lived a righteous life. Yet, he was subjected to severe trials—loss of wealth, the death of his children, and physical suffering. Despite these overwhelming hardships, Job's love for God remained steadfast. In Job 1:21, he famously declares, "The Lord gave, and the Lord has taken away; blessed be the name of the Lord." Job's love for God was not contingent on his circumstances; it was rooted in a deep, unwavering trust in God's character.

Similarly, in our relationships with others, love is often tested by difficult circumstances. Consider a marriage facing the strain of financial difficulties, or a friendship tested by betrayal. In these moments, love is challenged to go beyond mere emotion and become an intentional, sacrificial act of the will. It is easy to love when things are going well, but true love is revealed when it endures in the face of adversity.

The Apostle Paul, in his famous discourse on love in 1 Corinthians 13, describes love as patient, kind, and enduring. He writes, "Love bears all things, believes all things, hopes all things, endures all things" (1 Corinthians 13:7). This description of love is not abstract; it is practical and grounded in the reality of trials. Love that bears, believes, hopes, and endures is love that has been tested and proven true.

The Strengthening of Love Through Trials

While trials test the strength of love, they also have the potential to strengthen it. Just as physical exercise strengthens muscles, so too do spiritual and emotional trials have the potential to strengthen our capacity to love. This strengthening occurs as we learn to rely more on God's love for us and less on our own strength.

One of the ways trials strengthen love is by deepening our empathy and compassion for others. When we endure suffering, we become more attuned to the suffering of those around us. We begin to understand their pain on a deeper level, and this understanding fuels our love and compassion for them. The Apostle Paul writes in 2 Corinthians 1:3-4, "Blessed be the God and Father of our Lord Jesus Christ, the Father of mercies and God of all comfort, who comforts us in all our affliction, so that we may be able to comfort those who are in any affliction, with the comfort with which we ourselves are comforted by God." Our trials enable us to comfort others with the same comfort we have received from God, thereby strengthening the bonds of love within the Christian community.

Trials also strengthen love by stripping away the superficial and revealing what is truly important. In the midst of trials, we often find that many of the things we once valued—material possessions, status, or personal comfort—pale in comparison to the relationships and connections we share with others. This realization helps us to prioritize love over lesser pursuits. The things of this world may fade, but love endures. As Paul writes in 1 Corinthians 13:13, "So now faith, hope, and love abide, these three; but the greatest of these is love."

Moreover, trials teach us the importance of perseverance in love. In a culture that often promotes instant gratification and disposable relationships, the call to persevere in love can be countercultural. Yet, it is precisely through perseverance that love is refined and strengthened. James 1:4 encourages us to "let perseverance finish its work so that you may be mature and complete, not lacking anything." Perseverance in love leads to maturity and completeness, both in our relationships with others and in our relationship with God.

The Role of Faith in Enduring Love

Faith and love are inextricably linked in the Christian life. Faith provides the foundation for love, while love is the evidence of faith. When trials come, it is faith that sustains love, enabling it to endure and even flourish in the face of adversity.

James 1:12 speaks to the reward of enduring trials: "Blessed is the man who remains steadfast under trial, for when he has stood the test he will receive the crown of life, which God has promised to those who love him." The crown of life is a symbol of the eternal reward that awaits those who remain faithful to God through trials. It is a reminder that our love for God and for others is not in vain; it is part of the larger story of God's redemptive work in the world.

Faith gives us the strength to love even when it is difficult. It reminds us that God's love for us is steadfast and unchanging, even in the midst of our trials. When we are tempted to give up on love—whether because of weariness, hurt, or fear—faith calls us to press on, trusting that God's love will sustain us.

The writer of Hebrews encourages believers to "run with endurance the race that is set before us, looking to Jesus, the founder and perfecter of our faith" (Hebrews 12:1-2). Jesus is both the source and the example of enduring love. His love for us led Him to the cross, where He endured unimaginable suffering for our sake. His love did not waver, even in the face of betrayal, abandonment, and death. When we look to Jesus, we find the strength and courage to love others as He has loved us.

Faith also gives us hope in the midst of trials. It assures us that our trials are not meaningless but are being used by God to accomplish His purposes in our lives. As Paul writes in Romans 8:28, "And we know that in all things God works for the good of those who love him, who have been called according to his purpose." This hope enables us to endure trials with a sense of purpose, knowing that God is at work even in the most difficult circumstances.

The Example of Christ's Enduring Love

The ultimate example of love enduring through trials is found in the life of Jesus Christ. Throughout His earthly ministry, Jesus faced numerous trials—temptation, rejection, opposition, and ultimately, crucifixion. Yet, His love for humanity never wavered. It was a love that was tested and proven true, even in the face of the greatest suffering.

In the Garden of Gethsemane, on the night before His crucifixion, Jesus experienced deep anguish as He contemplated the suffering that lay ahead. He prayed, "My Father, if it be possible, let this cup pass from me; nevertheless, not as I will, but as you will" (Matthew 26:39). In this moment of trial, Jesus' love for the Father and for humanity was tested. Yet, His love endured. He chose to submit to the Father's will, knowing that His sacrifice was necessary for the salvation of the world.

On the cross, Jesus' love was tested to the utmost. He was mocked, beaten, and nailed to a cross—a punishment reserved for the worst of criminals. Yet, even in the midst of His suffering, His love remained steadfast. He prayed for those who crucified Him, saying, "Father, forgive them, for they know not what they do" (Luke 23:34). His love was not diminished by the pain and humiliation He endured; it was magnified.

The resurrection of Jesus is the ultimate testament to the enduring power of love. Death could not defeat Him, and the grave could not hold Him. His love triumphed over sin, death, and all the powers of darkness. This is the love that sustains us in our trials—the love that conquered death and brought us life.

As followers of Christ, we are called to model our love after His. This means that our love must be willing to endure trials, to forgive those who hurt us, and to sacrifice for the sake of others. It is a love that is not dependent on circumstances but is rooted in the unchanging love of God.

Practical Ways to Cultivate Enduring Love

Cultivating a love that endures through trials is not something that happens automatically; it requires intentionality and practice. Here are some practical ways to develop and strengthen enduring love in your life:

1. Deepen Your Relationship with God: The foundation of enduring love is a deep, personal relationship with God. Spend time in prayer, worship, and meditation on Scripture. Allow God's love to fill your heart and overflow into your relationships with others.

2. Practice Forgiveness: Trials often involve hurt and betrayal. Choosing to forgive, even when it is difficult, is a powerful way to cultivate enduring love. Remember that forgiveness is not about condoning wrongdoing but about releasing the burden of bitterness and allowing love to heal.

3. Cultivate Patience: Enduring love requires patience, especially in difficult situations. Practice patience by intentionally slowing down, being present in the moment, and giving others the grace to grow and change.

4. Seek Support from the Christian Community: Trials are easier to bear when we have the support of others. Surround yourself with a community of believers who can encourage, pray for, and walk alongside you in your journey.

5. Serve Others: Acts of service are a tangible expression of love, especially in the midst of trials. Look for opportunities to serve those around you, even when you are going through difficulties yourself. Serving others shifts the focus away from your own struggles and helps to build a sense of connection and purpose.

6. Keep an Eternal Perspective: Remember that this life is not all there is. The trials we face are temporary, but the love we cultivate has eternal significance. Keeping an eternal perspective helps to sustain love through the ups and downs of life.

7. Practice Gratitude: Cultivating a heart of gratitude, even in the midst of trials, can strengthen your capacity to love. Focus on the blessings in your life, and thank God for His faithfulness. Gratitude shifts your focus from what is lacking to what is present, allowing love to flourish.

8. Reflect on Christ's Sacrifice: Regularly meditate on the sacrifice of Christ and the love He demonstrated on the cross. Allow His example to inspire and motivate you to love others sacrificially and endure through trials.

9. Be Open to Growth: Trials are opportunities for growth, both in your faith and in your ability to love. Be open to the lessons that God wants to teach you through your trials, and allow Him to shape and refine your character.

10. Pray for Endurance: Finally, pray for the strength and endurance to love others through trials. Ask God to fill you with His love and empower you to persevere in love, no matter what challenges you face.

Conclusion

Love in the face of trials is not a passive emotion; it is an active, intentional choice to remain steadfast in our commitment to others, even when it is difficult. The trials we face in life are not obstacles to love but opportunities to strengthen and deepen our love. They test the authenticity of our love, refine it, and ultimately, make it more resilient.

As Christians, we are called to model our love after the love of Christ—a love that endured the ultimate trial for our sake. His example teaches us that true love is sacrificial, patient, and enduring. It is a love that does not give up in the face of adversity but perseveres with faith and hope.

May we, like the Apostle James, count it all joy when we face trials, knowing that the testing of our love produces endurance. And may we remain steadfast in our love, trusting that God is at work in us, refining our love and preparing us for the crown of life that He has promised to those who love Him.

In the end, it is love that will endure. The trials of this life are temporary, but the love we cultivate will last for eternity. Let us, therefore, love one another with the enduring love of Christ, knowing that "love never ends" (1 Corinthians 13:8).

Chapter 4: Forgiveness as an Act of Love

Introduction

Forgiveness is one of the most powerful and transformative acts of love. It is also one of the most challenging. In a world where hurt, betrayal, and injustice are common experiences, the call to forgive can seem overwhelming and even unreasonable. Yet, forgiveness is at the heart of the Christian faith. It is a central theme in the teachings of Jesus, and it is a reflection of the divine love that God extends to each of us. In Ephesians 4:32, the Apostle Paul writes, "Be kind to one another, tenderhearted, forgiving one another, as God in Christ forgave you." This verse captures the essence of forgiveness as an act of love—a love that mirrors the forgiveness we have received from God.

In this chapter, we will delve into the importance of forgiveness in relationships, exploring its theological significance, its challenges, and its profound impact on both the forgiver and the forgiven. We will examine how forgiveness reflects divine love and consider practical ways to cultivate a forgiving heart.

The Theological Foundation of Forgiveness

Forgiveness is not merely a social or psychological concept; it is deeply rooted in the character of God and the narrative of Scripture. The Bible presents forgiveness as an essential aspect of God's relationship with humanity. From the Old Testament to the New, the theme of forgiveness is woven throughout the biblical story, culminating in the life, death, and resurrection of Jesus Christ.

In the Old Testament, the concept of forgiveness is closely tied to the sacrificial system. The Law of Moses provided a framework for the Israelites to seek forgiveness through the offering of sacrifices. These sacrifices were a means of atonement, allowing the people to be reconciled to God after they had sinned. However, the sacrificial system was not an end in itself; it pointed to the need for a deeper, more permanent solution to the problem of sin.

The prophets of the Old Testament, such as Isaiah and Jeremiah, spoke of a coming Messiah who would bring true forgiveness and reconciliation. Isaiah 53:5-6 prophesies about the suffering servant who would bear the sins of many: "But he was pierced for our transgressions; he was crushed for our iniquities;

the punishment that brought us peace was on him, and by his wounds we are healed. We all, like sheep, have gone astray, each of us has turned to our own way; and the Lord has laid on him the iniquity of us all."

In the New Testament, the arrival of Jesus Christ fulfills these prophetic promises. Jesus is the Lamb of God who takes away the sin of the world (John 1:29). His sacrificial death on the cross is the ultimate act of forgiveness. Through His death and resurrection, Jesus offers forgiveness to all who believe in Him, reconciling them to God and restoring their relationship with the Father.

The forgiveness that Jesus offers is not earned; it is a gift of grace. Ephesians 2:8-9 reminds us, "For it is by grace you have been saved, through faith—and this is not from yourselves, it is the gift of God—not by works, so that no one can boast." This grace is the foundation of our salvation, and it is also the model for how we are to forgive others. Just as God has freely forgiven us, we are called to extend that same forgiveness to those who have wronged us.

Forgiveness as a Reflection of Divine Love

Forgiveness is a profound expression of love because it reflects the nature of God's love for us. God's love is unconditional, sacrificial, and redemptive. It is a love that reaches out to us even when we are unworthy, offering us grace and mercy instead of condemnation.

When we forgive others, we participate in this divine love. Forgiveness is an act of grace that transcends the natural human response to hurt and injustice. It is a choice to let go of the desire for revenge or retribution and instead offer compassion and mercy. This is not an easy choice, but it is one that reflects the heart of God.

In Matthew 18:21-22, Peter asks Jesus, "Lord, how many times shall I forgive my brother or sister who sins against me? Up to seven times?" Jesus responds, "I tell you, not seven times, but seventy-seven times." This response underscores the limitless nature of forgiveness in the kingdom of God. Jesus is not suggesting that we keep a tally of offenses but rather that our forgiveness should be boundless, just as God's forgiveness is boundless.

Forgiveness also reflects divine love in its power to bring healing and restoration. When we forgive, we open the door to reconciliation and the possibility of renewed relationships. This is the essence of God's redemptive love—a love that heals the broken, restores the fallen, and makes all things new.

The Challenges of Forgiveness

While forgiveness is a beautiful and powerful act of love, it is also one of the most difficult. The challenge of forgiveness lies in the reality of pain and the deep wounds that others can inflict on us. Betrayal, rejection, abuse, and injustice are not easily forgiven. The human response to such hurts is often anger, resentment, and a desire for justice or revenge.

These responses are understandable, and they reflect the real pain that comes from being wronged. However, they also have the potential to trap us in a cycle of bitterness and unforgiveness. When we hold on to anger and resentment, we carry the burden of the offense with us, allowing it to continue to hurt us long after the original act has occurred. Unforgiveness can become a prison that keeps us bound to the past, preventing us from moving forward and experiencing the fullness of life that God desires for us.

Jesus understood the difficulty of forgiveness, and He addressed it in His teachings. In the Sermon on the Mount, Jesus says, "You have heard that it was said, 'Love your neighbor and hate your enemy.' But I tell you, love your enemies and pray for those who persecute you, that you may be children of your Father in heaven" (Matthew 5:43-45). This teaching challenges us to go beyond our natural inclinations and to respond to hurt with love and forgiveness.

The difficulty of forgiveness is also acknowledged in the parable of the unforgiving servant (Matthew 18:23-35). In this parable, a servant who is forgiven a massive debt by his master refuses to forgive a fellow servant who owes him a much smaller debt. When the master learns of this, he is outraged and has the unforgiving servant thrown into prison. Jesus concludes the parable with a stern warning: "This is how my heavenly Father will treat each of you unless you forgive your brother or sister from your heart" (Matthew 18:35).

This parable highlights the seriousness of unforgiveness and the expectation that those who have received forgiveness must also extend it to others. It also illustrates the destructive nature of unforgiveness—it not only harms the person who refuses to forgive but also disrupts relationships and community.

The Process of Forgiveness

Forgiveness is often described as a process rather than a one-time event. This process can be lengthy and complex, especially when the hurt is deep. It involves several stages, each of which requires intentionality and a willingness to allow God to work in our hearts.

1. Acknowledgment of the Hurt: The first step in the process of forgiveness is acknowledging the hurt that has been done. This involves being honest about the pain and allowing yourself to feel the emotions that come with it—anger, sadness, betrayal, or disappointment. It is important not to rush past this step, as denying or minimizing the hurt can hinder the process of true forgiveness.

2. Choosing to Forgive: Forgiveness begins with a decision. It is a conscious choice to let go of the desire for revenge or retribution and to extend grace instead. This decision may need to be repeated many times, especially if the pain resurfaces. Forgiveness is not a one-time act but a continual choice to walk in love and grace.

3. Releasing the Offender: Forgiveness involves releasing the offender from the debt that they owe you. This means letting go of the expectation that they will make things right or that they will suffer consequences for their actions. It is entrusting them to God, who is the ultimate judge and who will deal with them according to His justice and mercy.

4. Seeking Healing: Forgiveness is not synonymous with healing, but it opens the door for healing to take place. Healing may involve processing the hurt with a trusted friend or counselor, praying for God's comfort and strength, and allowing time for the wound to mend. Healing is a journey, and it may take time, but forgiveness is an essential part of that journey.

5. Pursuing Reconciliation: Reconciliation is the restoration of a broken relationship. While forgiveness is a necessary step toward reconciliation, it does not always lead to it. Reconciliation requires both parties to be willing to rebuild trust and repair the relationship. In some cases, reconciliation may not be possible or advisable, especially if the offender is unrepentant or if the relationship is unsafe. However, the goal of forgiveness is always to move toward reconciliation, even if it is not fully realized.

6. Continuing in Forgiveness: Forgiveness is an ongoing process. The enemy may try to bring up the past and tempt you to hold on to bitterness

or resentment. In those moments, it is important to reaffirm your decision to forgive and to ask God for the grace to continue walking in forgiveness. Remember that forgiveness is a journey, and it may require ongoing effort and prayer.

Forgiveness in Relationships

Forgiveness is essential to healthy relationships. In any relationship—whether it is a marriage, a friendship, or a family bond—there will inevitably be misunderstandings, disagreements, and offenses. How we respond to these offenses can either strengthen or weaken the relationship.

Forgiveness allows us to move past the hurt and rebuild trust. It creates an environment where love can flourish and where both parties can grow together. In contrast, unforgiveness breeds resentment, bitterness, and division. It creates walls between people and can ultimately destroy relationships.

In marriage, forgiveness is particularly important. The intimacy and vulnerability of marriage make it fertile ground for both deep love and deep hurt. Spouses may unintentionally or intentionally hurt each other through words, actions, or neglect. Without forgiveness, these hurts can accumulate and create a rift in the relationship. But when forgiveness is practiced regularly, it fosters an atmosphere of grace and allows the marriage to grow stronger through challenges.

Friendships also require forgiveness to thrive. True friendship involves being open and honest with one another, which can sometimes lead to conflict. Forgiveness enables friends to address issues, resolve conflicts, and continue to support and care for one another. It is a key component of lasting and meaningful friendships.

In families, forgiveness is vital for maintaining harmony and unity. Family members often know each other's weaknesses and can easily hurt one another. Forgiveness helps to maintain the bonds of love and respect, even when there are disagreements or misunderstandings. It allows family members to move past conflicts and to continue to love and support one another.

Forgiveness also plays a critical role in the broader Christian community. The church is called to be a place of love, grace, and reconciliation. When offenses occur within the church, forgiveness is essential for maintaining unity and fellowship. Paul writes in Colossians 3:13, "Bear with each other and forgive one another if any of you has a grievance against someone. Forgive as the Lord forgave you." This call to forgiveness is foundational to the health and witness of the church.

The Power of Forgiveness

Forgiveness is not only an act of love; it is also a powerful force for change and transformation. It has the ability to break the cycle of hurt and retaliation, to bring healing to deep wounds, and to restore relationships.

One of the most profound examples of the power of forgiveness is found in the story of Joseph in the Old Testament. Joseph was betrayed by his brothers, who sold him into slavery out of jealousy. He endured years of hardship, including false accusations and imprisonment. Yet, when he was reunited with his brothers, Joseph chose to forgive them. In Genesis 50:20, he says, "You intended to harm me, but God intended it for good to accomplish what is now being done, the saving of many lives." Joseph's forgiveness not only restored his relationship with his brothers but also allowed God's plan for the salvation of many people to be fulfilled.

Forgiveness also has the power to transform the heart of the forgiver. When we choose to forgive, we release the burden of anger and bitterness that weighs us down. We experience the freedom that comes from letting go of the offense and entrusting it to God. This freedom allows us to live more fully in the present and to engage more deeply in our relationships.

Moreover, forgiveness has the power to transform the heart of the offender. When someone is genuinely forgiven, it can lead to repentance and change. The grace that is extended through forgiveness can soften even the hardest of hearts and open the door for reconciliation and new beginnings.

The power of forgiveness is also evident in the larger society. Throughout history, movements of forgiveness and reconciliation have brought about significant social change. One of the most notable examples is the Truth and Reconciliation Commission in South Africa, which was established after the end of apartheid. The commission provided a platform for victims and perpetrators of human rights violations to share their stories, seek forgiveness, and work toward healing and reconciliation. This process of forgiveness played a critical role in the nation's journey toward peace and unity.

Practical Ways to Cultivate Forgiveness

Cultivating a heart of forgiveness requires intentionality and a reliance on God's grace. Here are some practical ways to develop and practice forgiveness in your life:

1. Pray for a Forgiving Heart: Begin by asking God to help you cultivate a heart of forgiveness. Pray for the strength to forgive those who have hurt you and for the grace to extend forgiveness even when it is difficult.

2. Reflect on God's Forgiveness: Regularly meditate on the forgiveness that God has extended to you through Jesus Christ. Reflecting on God's grace and mercy toward you can help you to extend that same grace and mercy to others.

3. Choose to Forgive: Remember that forgiveness is a choice, not a feeling. Even if you do not feel like forgiving, make the decision to forgive and trust God to work in your heart.

4. Practice Empathy: Try to put yourself in the shoes of the person who has hurt you. Consider what might have led them to act the way they did. Practicing empathy can help to soften your heart and make forgiveness more attainable.

5. Release the Offense: Let go of the desire for revenge or retribution. Release the offense to God and trust Him to deal with it according to His justice and mercy.

6. Seek Support: Forgiveness can be difficult to navigate on your own. Seek support from a trusted friend, counselor, or pastor who can help you process your hurt and encourage you to forgive.

7. Practice Gratitude: Cultivating a heart of gratitude can help to shift your focus from the hurt to the blessings in your life. Gratitude can create a more positive and forgiving mindset.

8. Set Boundaries: Forgiveness does not mean allowing someone to continue to hurt you. It is important to set healthy boundaries in relationships where necessary. Forgiveness and boundaries can coexist and are both important for healthy relationships.

9. Pursue Reconciliation When Possible: If it is safe and appropriate, seek to reconcile with the person who has hurt you. Be open to the possibility of rebuilding trust and restoring the relationship.

10. Trust in God's Justice: Remember that God is the ultimate judge, and He will deal with all wrongs according to His justice. Trusting in God's justice allows you to release the offense and focus on healing and moving forward.

Conclusion

Forgiveness is one of the most profound and powerful expressions of love. It is a reflection of the divine love that God extends to us—a love that is unconditional, sacrificial, and redemptive. While forgiveness can be challenging, it is essential for healthy relationships, personal healing, and spiritual growth.

As we forgive others, we participate in the love and grace of God, allowing His forgiveness to flow through us and into our relationships. Forgiveness has the power to break the cycle of hurt and bitterness, to bring healing and restoration, and to transform both the forgiver and the forgiven.

May we, as followers of Christ, be people who forgive as God has forgiven us. May we extend grace and mercy to those who have wronged us, trusting in God's justice and allowing His love to guide us. And may we experience the freedom, peace, and healing that come from living a life marked by forgiveness—a life that reflects the heart of God.

Chapter 5: Patience and Long-Suffering

Introduction

Patience is a virtue that is universally admired but often difficult to practice. In our fast-paced, instant-gratification culture, waiting has become something to be avoided at all costs. Yet, within the Christian faith, patience, often coupled with long-suffering, is not just a necessary inconvenience but a profound expression of love and faith. In 1 Corinthians 13:4, the Apostle Paul writes, "Love is patient, love is kind." This simple yet profound statement places patience at the very heart of love, suggesting that true love cannot exist without it.

In this chapter, we will explore the role of patience and long-suffering in the life of a believer, especially as it pertains to love. We will reflect on the theological significance of patience, the challenges it presents, and how it intertwines with faith in God's timing. Furthermore, we will delve into practical ways to cultivate patience and long-suffering in our daily lives, demonstrating how these qualities are essential for deep, enduring relationships and a mature faith.

The Theological Significance of Patience

Patience is more than just the ability to wait; it is a reflection of God's character and a testament to our trust in Him. The Bible frequently describes God as patient and long-suffering. In Exodus 34:6, God reveals Himself to Moses by proclaiming, "The Lord, the Lord, a God merciful and gracious, slow to anger, and abounding in steadfast love and faithfulness." Here, God's patience is highlighted as a key aspect of His nature.

This divine patience is not passive or indifferent; it is active and purposeful. God's patience is an expression of His mercy and love, as He waits for humanity to turn back to Him. The Apostle Peter echoes this in 2 Peter 3:9, where he writes, "The Lord is not slow in keeping his promise, as some understand slowness. Instead, he is patient with you, not wanting anyone to perish, but everyone to come to repentance." God's patience is rooted in His desire for our redemption and reconciliation with Him.

As bearers of God's image, we are called to reflect this divine patience in our own lives. Patience, therefore, is not just a passive waiting but an active engagement in love and faith. It is the willingness to endure difficulties, delays, and disappointments without losing hope or giving in to frustration. In this sense, patience is deeply intertwined with love, as it allows us to bear with one another, forgive offenses, and continue loving even when it is challenging.

Patience as an Expression of Love

When Paul writes that "love is patient" in 1 Corinthians 13:4, he is speaking to the enduring, long-suffering nature of true love. Patience in love means more than just tolerating someone's faults or waiting for them to change. It is about being committed to the well-being of another person, even when the journey is slow, difficult, or fraught with challenges.

In relationships, whether romantic, familial, or friendships, patience is essential for sustaining and deepening the bond between individuals. Every relationship will face trials—misunderstandings, unmet expectations, and personal growth that occurs at different paces. Patience allows love to persevere through these challenges, providing the space and grace needed for healing, growth, and reconciliation.

One of the most poignant examples of patience in love is found in the story of Hosea and Gomer in the Old Testament. Hosea, a prophet, was commanded by God to marry Gomer, a woman who would be unfaithful to him. Despite her repeated betrayals, Hosea patiently loved Gomer, redeeming her from her life of sin and restoring her to himself. This story is not only a testament to Hosea's patience and long-suffering love but also a powerful metaphor for God's enduring love for His people. Like Hosea, God patiently waits for us, forgives us, and continually draws us back to Himself, despite our unfaithfulness.

Patience in love also involves a willingness to wait on God's timing. In a world that often demands immediate results, waiting can feel like a waste of time or a sign of weakness. However, in the Christian life, waiting is an act of faith. It is a declaration that we trust God's plan and His timing, even when we do not understand it. This kind of patience requires humility, as we acknowledge that God's ways are higher than our ways, and His thoughts are higher than our thoughts (Isaiah 55:9).

Challenges to Patience and Long-Suffering

While patience is a virtue, it is not one that comes easily. There are several challenges to practicing patience and long-suffering, particularly in the context of relationships and faith.

1. Impatience and the Desire for Control: One of the primary challenges to patience is our natural inclination toward impatience and the desire to control our circumstances. When we are faced with delays or difficulties, our instinct is often to try to fix the situation or to push for a resolution. This desire for control can lead to frustration and anxiety, especially when things do not go according to our plans.

2. Cultural Pressures: We live in a culture that values speed, efficiency, and instant gratification. From fast food to high-speed internet, we are conditioned to expect immediate results. This cultural mindset can make it difficult to embrace the slow, deliberate process of patience. We may feel pressure to move quickly in relationships, to achieve success rapidly, or to make decisions without waiting for God's guidance.

3. Fear of Vulnerability: Patience often requires us to be vulnerable—to admit that we do not have all the answers, to wait in uncertainty, and to trust in someone else. This vulnerability can be uncomfortable and even frightening. We may fear that waiting will result in disappointment, or that being patient with someone will leave us open to being hurt or taken advantage of.

4. The Pain of Long-Suffering: Long-suffering, by its very definition, involves enduring pain or hardship for an extended period. Whether it is waiting for a loved one to change, enduring a chronic illness, or holding on to hope in the face of unrelenting challenges, long-suffering is difficult and can be emotionally and spiritually draining.

5. Doubt and Discouragement: When we are in the midst of a long trial, it is easy to become discouraged and to doubt whether our patience will ever be rewarded. We may question whether God is really at work, whether things will ever change, or whether our waiting is in vain. This doubt can erode our patience and lead us to give up on love, faith, or hope.

Patience and Faith in God's Timing

Patience is closely linked with faith, particularly faith in God's timing. The Bible is full of stories of people who had to wait—sometimes for years or even decades—before they saw the fulfillment of God's promises. Abraham and Sarah waited for the birth of Isaac, Joseph waited in prison before being elevated to power in Egypt, and the Israelites waited for centuries for the coming of the Messiah.

In each of these stories, waiting was not just a passive activity; it was an active demonstration of faith. Abraham and Sarah, despite their advanced age, believed that God would fulfill His promise of a son. Joseph, despite his unjust imprisonment, remained faithful to God and trusted in His plan. The Israelites, despite their long history of suffering and exile, held on to the hope of a Savior.

Waiting on God's timing requires us to trust that His plan is perfect and that He knows what is best for us. This trust is not always easy, especially when we are faced with delays, setbacks, or uncertainty. However, the Bible assures us that God's timing is always right. Ecclesiastes 3:11 tells us, "He has made everything beautiful in its time." This verse reminds us that God is at work, even when we cannot see it, and that His timing is designed to bring about the best possible outcome.

Patience in God's timing also involves surrendering our own plans and desires to Him. Proverbs 3:5-6 encourages us to "Trust in the Lord with all your heart and lean not on your own understanding; in all your ways submit to him, and he will make your paths straight." This submission requires us to let go of our need for control and to trust that God's ways are higher and better than our own.

One of the most challenging aspects of waiting on God's timing is the need for perseverance. James 1:2-4 encourages believers to "Consider it pure joy, my brothers and sisters, whenever you face trials of many kinds, because you know that the testing of your faith produces perseverance. Let perseverance finish its work so that you may be mature and complete, not lacking anything." Perseverance is the ability to keep going, even when the journey is long and difficult. It is the willingness to endure, to hold on to faith, and to continue trusting in God, even when the outcome is uncertain.

The Role of Long-Suffering in Love

Long-suffering, or the ability to endure hardship and pain over an extended period, is an essential aspect of love. It is closely related to patience but carries the added dimension of enduring suffering for the sake of love.

In relationships, long-suffering is the willingness to remain committed to someone, even when the relationship is difficult or painful. This could mean standing by a spouse who is struggling with addiction, being patient with a child who is going through a rebellious phase, or continuing to love and care for a friend who is dealing with depression. Long-suffering is not about enabling harmful behavior but about choosing to love someone through their struggles, with the hope of restoration and healing.

The ultimate example of long-suffering love is found in Jesus Christ. Throughout His ministry, Jesus demonstrated long-suffering in His interactions with people. He was patient with His disciples, even when they were slow to understand His teachings. He showed compassion to the crowds, even when they demanded more from Him than He could physically give. And most importantly, He endured the suffering of the cross out of love for humanity.

Hebrews 12:2 encourages believers to "fix our eyes on Jesus, the pioneer and perfecter of faith. For the joy set before him, he endured the cross, scorning its shame, and sat down at the right hand of the throne of God." Jesus' long-suffering love was motivated by the joy of redeeming humanity and restoring us to a relationship with God. His willingness to endure the cross is the ultimate act of love and a model for how we are to love others.

Long-suffering in love also involves forgiveness. In relationships, there will be times when we are hurt, disappointed, or betrayed by those we love. Long-suffering love chooses to forgive, even when the hurt is deep and the wound is fresh. It recognizes that forgiveness is not about condoning wrongdoing but about freeing ourselves from the burden of resentment and allowing love to heal.

Cultivating Patience and Long-Suffering in Daily Life

Cultivating patience and long-suffering requires intentional effort and a reliance on God's grace. Here are some practical ways to develop these qualities in your daily life:

1. Pray for Patience: Begin by asking God to help you cultivate a patient and long-suffering heart. Pray for the strength to endure difficulties, the grace to wait on His timing, and the love to bear with others.

2. Practice Mindfulness: Mindfulness is the practice of being fully present in the moment. It can help you to slow down, to be aware of your thoughts and emotions, and to respond to situations with patience rather than reacting impulsively.

3. Embrace Delays: Instead of seeing delays as a frustration, try to view them as opportunities to practice patience. Whether you are waiting in line, stuck in traffic, or facing a delay in a relationship or goal, use the time to pray, reflect, or simply be still.

4. Reflect on God's Patience: Regularly meditate on the patience and long-suffering of God, both in Scripture and in your own life. Reflect on how God has been patient with you, and allow His example to inspire you to be patient with others.

5. Set Realistic Expectations: Patience often falters when our expectations are unrealistic. Set realistic expectations for yourself, for others, and for God's timing. Recognize that growth, change, and healing take time.

6. Focus on the Bigger Picture: When you are tempted to lose patience, try to step back and see the bigger picture. Consider how your current situation fits into God's larger plan for your life, and trust that He is at work, even in the waiting.

7. Foster a Spirit of Gratitude: Gratitude can help to cultivate patience by shifting your focus from what you lack to what you have. Regularly practice gratitude by thanking God for His blessings, even in the midst of trials.

8. Lean on Community: Surround yourself with a supportive community of believers who can encourage you in your journey of patience and long-suffering. Share your struggles with others, and allow them to pray for and support you.

9. Practice Self-Compassion: Be patient with yourself as you seek to cultivate patience and long-suffering. Recognize that growth is a process and that you will have moments of impatience and frustration. Extend grace to yourself, just as God extends grace to you.

10. Keep an Eternal Perspective: Remember that this life is not all there is. The trials and challenges we face are temporary, but the love we cultivate will last for eternity. Keeping an eternal perspective can help you to endure with patience and long-suffering.

The Fruit of Patience and Long-Suffering

The fruit of patience and long-suffering is evident in the transformation it brings to our lives and relationships. When we practice patience, we create an environment where love can flourish. We become more compassionate, more understanding, and more willing to forgive. Our relationships deepen as we learn to bear with one another, to wait on God's timing, and to trust in His plan.

Patience also produces spiritual maturity. James 1:4 tells us that perseverance "must finish its work so that you may be mature and complete, not lacking anything." As we endure trials with patience and long-suffering, we grow in our faith and become more like Christ. Our character is refined, our faith is strengthened, and we are better equipped to love others with the love of Christ.

In addition, patience and long-suffering bring peace. When we are able to wait on God's timing and to endure difficulties with grace, we experience a sense of peace that transcends our circumstances. This peace is a gift from God, and it allows us to remain steadfast in our love and faith, even in the midst of trials.

Conclusion

Patience and long-suffering are not just qualities to be admired from a distance; they are essential aspects of love and faith. They reflect the character of God, who is patient and long-suffering with us, and they enable us to love others with the same enduring love.

As we seek to cultivate patience and long-suffering in our lives, may we be inspired by the example of Christ, who endured the cross for the joy set before

Him. May we trust in God's timing, surrender our plans to Him, and wait with hope and faith for the fulfillment of His promises. And may our love, like God's love, be patient, kind, and enduring, reflecting the heart of our Savior in all that we do.

Chapter 6: The Covenant of Marriage

Introduction

Marriage is one of the most profound and sacred institutions established by God. It is a union that transcends mere human agreement, embodying a spiritual and covenantal bond that reflects God's relationship with His people. The concept of marriage as a covenant is deeply rooted in Scripture, with foundational texts such as Genesis 2:24, which states, "Therefore a man shall leave his father and mother and be joined to his wife, and they shall become one flesh," and Ephesians 5:31-32, where Paul echoes this verse and connects it to the mystery of Christ and the church. These passages reveal the divine intention behind marriage as a covenantal relationship, mirroring God's unwavering commitment to His people.

In this chapter, we will explore the concept of marriage as a covenant, examining its theological significance, its implications for marital love, and how it mirrors the sacred covenant between God and His people. We will delve into the biblical foundations of marriage, reflect on the responsibilities and commitments involved in a covenantal marriage, and consider practical ways to cultivate and sustain a covenantal relationship that honors God.

The Biblical Foundation of Marriage as a Covenant

The idea of marriage as a covenant is rooted in the earliest chapters of the Bible, where God establishes the first marriage between Adam and Eve. In Genesis 2:18, God declares, "It is not good that man should be alone; I will make him a helper comparable to him." God's creation of Eve from Adam's rib symbolizes the deep connection and unity that marriage is meant to embody. When Adam sees Eve, he recognizes her as "bone of my bones and flesh of my flesh" (Genesis 2:23), highlighting the intimate and inseparable bond that marriage creates.

The concept of "one flesh" in Genesis 2:24 is particularly significant in understanding marriage as a covenant. The phrase "one flesh" denotes a unity that goes beyond physical union; it signifies a deep, spiritual, and emotional oneness that is reflective of the covenantal relationship between God and His people. In marriage, two individuals become one in a way that mirrors the unity and commitment found in God's covenant with humanity.

The covenantal nature of marriage is further emphasized in the prophetic literature of the Old Testament, where God frequently uses the metaphor of marriage to describe His relationship with Israel. For example, in the book of Hosea, God instructs the prophet Hosea to marry a woman named Gomer, who is unfaithful to him, as a symbolic representation of Israel's unfaithfulness to God. Despite Gomer's infidelity, Hosea is called to love her and to take her back, reflecting God's steadfast love and covenantal faithfulness to Israel, even when they stray.

The concept of marriage as a covenant is also central in the New Testament, particularly in the writings of the Apostle Paul. In Ephesians 5:31-32, Paul quotes Genesis 2:24 and then adds, "This is a great mystery, but I speak concerning Christ and the church." Here, Paul reveals that marriage is not only a covenant between a man and a woman but also a reflection of the covenant between Christ and the church. Just as Christ loves the church and gave Himself for her, so too are husbands called to love their wives sacrificially. The wife's submission to her husband, in turn, reflects the church's submission to Christ. This mutual love and respect, grounded in the covenantal relationship, form the foundation of a God-honoring marriage.

The Sacredness of the Marital Covenant

Understanding marriage as a covenant elevates it beyond a mere contract or social arrangement. A contract is based on mutual benefits and can be dissolved if one party fails to uphold their end of the agreement. In contrast, a covenant is a sacred and binding commitment that is meant to endure, regardless of circumstances. It is a vow made before God and witnesses, signifying a lifelong commitment to love, honor, and cherish one another.

The sacredness of the marital covenant is rooted in the fact that it is established by God. In Mark 10:9, Jesus affirms this when He says, "Therefore what God has joined together, let no one separate." Marriage is not simply a human institution; it is a divine ordinance, established by God from the beginning of creation. This understanding places marriage in the realm of the holy, requiring reverence and intentionality in how it is approached and lived out.

In the Old Testament, covenants were often sealed with a ritual or sign, such as the cutting of animals or the exchange of vows. Similarly, the marriage covenant is sealed with vows made by the bride and groom, pledging their love and fidelity to one another. These vows are not just promises to one another but are also commitments made before God. As such, they carry a weight of responsibility and accountability.

The sacredness of the marital covenant also reflects the nature of God's covenant with His people. God's covenantal love is characterized by faithfulness, steadfastness, and unconditional love. Despite Israel's repeated unfaithfulness, God remained faithful to His covenant, demonstrating His unwavering commitment to His people. In the same way, the marital covenant calls for a commitment to love, honor, and remain faithful to one's spouse, regardless of the challenges that may arise.

Responsibilities and Commitments in a Covenant Marriage

A covenant marriage involves specific responsibilities and commitments that are essential for maintaining and nurturing the relationship. These responsibilities are not simply duties to be fulfilled but are expressions of love and devotion that reflect the covenantal nature of the relationship.

1. Mutual Love and Respect: Central to the covenant of marriage is the commitment to love and respect one another. In Ephesians 5:25, Paul instructs husbands to "love your wives, just as Christ also loved the church and gave Himself for her." This sacrificial love is the standard for husbands, requiring them to put the needs and well-being of their wives above their own. Similarly, wives are called to respect their husbands, as Paul writes in Ephesians 5:33, "Let the wife see that she respects her husband." Mutual love and respect are foundational to a healthy and God-honoring marriage, as they create an environment of trust, honor, and support.

2. Faithfulness and Loyalty: Faithfulness is a key component of the marital covenant. Just as God is faithful to His covenant with His people, so too are spouses called to be faithful to one another. This faithfulness is not limited to physical fidelity but also includes emotional, spiritual, and relational loyalty. It involves guarding one's heart, mind, and actions to ensure that the marriage

remains a priority and that no other person or thing takes precedence over the marital relationship.

3. Sacrifice and Service: Covenant marriage involves a willingness to sacrifice for the sake of the other. This sacrificial love is modeled after Christ's love for the church, as He gave Himself up for her. In practical terms, this means being willing to put one's own desires and needs aside for the sake of one's spouse. It involves serving one another with humility and grace, recognizing that marriage is not about what one can get out of it but about what one can give.

4. Forgiveness and Grace: No marriage is perfect, and there will inevitably be times when one or both spouses fall short of their commitments. In these moments, the covenantal nature of marriage calls for forgiveness and grace. Just as God forgives us and extends grace to us, so too are we called to forgive and extend grace to our spouse. This does not mean overlooking wrongdoing or ignoring issues but rather approaching them with a spirit of love and a desire for reconciliation.

5. Communication and Understanding: Effective communication is essential in a covenant marriage. It involves not only expressing one's own thoughts and feelings but also listening and seeking to understand the other person's perspective. Communication is the means by which love, respect, and mutual understanding are cultivated and maintained. It is through open and honest communication that spouses can address issues, resolve conflicts, and grow closer to one another.

6. Commitment to Growth: A covenant marriage is not static; it involves a commitment to ongoing growth, both individually and as a couple. This growth may involve spiritual development, emotional maturity, and relational skills. It requires a willingness to learn, adapt, and grow together, recognizing that marriage is a journey that requires continuous effort and intentionality.

7. Prayer and Spiritual Unity: A covenant marriage is rooted in a shared faith and commitment to God. Prayer is a vital component of this spiritual unity, as it strengthens the bond between spouses and deepens their relationship with God. Praying together and for one another fosters spiritual intimacy and aligns the marriage with God's purposes and plans. It is through prayer that spouses can seek God's guidance, wisdom, and strength for their marriage.

The Covenant of Marriage as a Reflection of God's Covenant with His People

One of the most profound aspects of marriage as a covenant is that it mirrors God's covenant with His people. Throughout Scripture, marriage is used as a metaphor for the relationship between God and His people, particularly in the prophetic books and in the New Testament.

In the book of Hosea, the prophet's marriage to Gomer serves as a powerful symbol of God's covenant with Israel. Despite Gomer's unfaithfulness, Hosea's commitment to her reflects God's steadfast love and faithfulness to His people, even when they are unfaithful. This narrative underscores the idea that God's love is not conditional or based on our actions but is a covenantal love that endures despite our shortcomings.

In the New Testament, Paul expands on this metaphor by comparing marriage to the relationship between Christ and the church. In Ephesians 5:25-27, Paul writes, "Husbands, love your wives, just as Christ also loved the church and gave Himself for her, that He might sanctify and cleanse her with the washing of water by the word, that He might present her to Himself a glorious church, not having spot or wrinkle or any such thing, but that she should be holy and without blemish." Here, Paul emphasizes the sacrificial and purifying nature of Christ's love for the church, which is to be reflected in the love of a husband for his wife.

This comparison between marriage and God's covenant with His people highlights several important truths about the nature of marital love:

1. Sacrificial Love: Just as Christ sacrificed Himself for the church, so too are spouses called to love sacrificially. This involves putting the needs and well-being of one's spouse above one's own and being willing to make sacrifices for the sake of the relationship.

2. Sanctifying Love: In the same way that Christ's love sanctifies and purifies the church, marital love has the potential to sanctify and strengthen both individuals. This sanctifying love involves encouraging one another in the faith, holding each other accountable, and supporting one another's spiritual growth.

3. Unconditional Love: God's covenantal love for His people is unconditional, meaning it is not based on what we do but on who God is.

Similarly, marital love is not conditional on the other person's actions or behavior but is rooted in the covenantal commitment to love, honor, and cherish one another.

4. Enduring Love: God's covenant with His people is eternal, and His love endures forever. In the same way, the marital covenant is meant to be a lifelong commitment, enduring through all seasons of life, both good and bad.

5. Covenantal Faithfulness: Just as God is faithful to His covenant, spouses are called to be faithful to one another. This faithfulness is not just about avoiding infidelity but about being committed to the marriage, even when it is difficult. It involves being loyal, trustworthy, and dependable, just as God is with us.

Practical Ways to Cultivate a Covenant Marriage

Cultivating a covenant marriage requires intentionality, effort, and a reliance on God's grace. Here are some practical ways to nurture and sustain a covenantal relationship that honors God:

1. Regularly Renew Your Vows: Take time to regularly renew your marriage vows, either privately or in a formal ceremony. This practice can serve as a reminder of the covenantal commitment you made to one another and to God. It can also help to reinforce the importance of your marriage and the sacredness of your vows.

2. Prioritize Your Marriage: In the busyness of life, it can be easy for marriage to take a backseat to other responsibilities. However, a covenant marriage requires that you prioritize your relationship with your spouse. This means setting aside regular time to connect, communicate, and spend quality time together. It also means being intentional about protecting your marriage from outside distractions and influences.

3. Practice Sacrificial Love: Look for ways to practice sacrificial love in your marriage. This could involve making small sacrifices, such as giving up your preferences for the sake of your spouse, or larger sacrifices, such as supporting your spouse in a difficult decision or career change. Sacrificial love is about putting your spouse's needs and well-being above your own.

4. Seek Reconciliation and Forgiveness: When conflicts arise in your marriage, be quick to seek reconciliation and to offer forgiveness. Remember

that forgiveness is a key component of a covenant marriage, and it is essential for maintaining unity and peace in the relationship. Be willing to humble yourself, to apologize when necessary, and to extend grace to your spouse.

5. Cultivate Spiritual Unity: A covenant marriage is rooted in a shared faith and commitment to God. Cultivate spiritual unity by praying together, studying Scripture together, and participating in church and ministry activities as a couple. Spiritual unity strengthens the bond between spouses and aligns the marriage with God's purposes.

6. Communicate Openly and Honestly: Effective communication is essential for a healthy covenant marriage. Make it a priority to communicate openly and honestly with your spouse about your thoughts, feelings, and needs. Listen actively and seek to understand your spouse's perspective. Communication fosters trust, intimacy, and mutual understanding.

7. Invest in Your Marriage: Just as you would invest in your career or personal growth, it is important to invest in your marriage. This could involve attending marriage workshops or retreats, reading books on marriage, or seeking counseling when needed. Investing in your marriage demonstrates a commitment to its growth and well-being.

8. Practice Gratitude and Appreciation: Regularly express gratitude and appreciation for your spouse. Acknowledge the ways in which they contribute to the marriage and the qualities that you admire in them. Gratitude fosters a positive and loving atmosphere in the marriage and helps to strengthen the bond between spouses.

9. Keep the Covenant at the Center: Always remember that your marriage is a covenant, not just a contract or agreement. Keep the covenant at the center of your relationship by regularly reflecting on its significance and by making decisions that honor the sacredness of your vows.

10. Trust in God's Grace: Finally, remember that a covenant marriage is not sustained by human effort alone but by God's grace. Trust in God's grace to strengthen, sustain, and bless your marriage. Pray for His guidance, wisdom, and love to be evident in your relationship, and rely on His strength in times of difficulty.

Conclusion

The covenant of marriage is a sacred and profound institution, established by God as a reflection of His covenantal love for His people. It is a relationship that transcends mere human agreement, embodying a spiritual and covenantal bond that mirrors the unwavering commitment of God to His people. Understanding marriage as a covenant elevates it to a place of reverence and intentionality, requiring mutual love, respect, faithfulness, and sacrifice.

As we seek to live out the covenant of marriage, may we be inspired by the example of Christ and His love for the church. May we cultivate a marriage that honors God, reflects His covenantal love, and serves as a testimony to His grace and faithfulness. And may our marriages be a source of blessing, not only to one another but also to those around us, as we demonstrate the beauty and sacredness of the covenant of marriage.

Chapter 7: The Role of Prayer in Love

Introduction

Prayer is the lifeblood of the Christian faith, a vital communication channel between humanity and God. It is through prayer that we express our deepest needs, seek guidance, and align our hearts with God's will. In the context of love and relationships, prayer plays an indispensable role in nurturing, sustaining, and deepening the bond between individuals. The Apostle Paul, in his letter to the Philippians, offers a profound insight into the power of prayer: "Do not be anxious about anything, but in every situation, by prayer and petition, with thanksgiving, present your requests to God. And the peace of God, which transcends all understanding, will guard your hearts and your minds in Christ Jesus" (Philippians 4:6-7). This passage emphasizes the importance of bringing every aspect of our lives, including our relationships, before God in prayer.

In this chapter, we will explore the role of prayer in maintaining and strengthening a loving relationship. We will reflect on the theological significance of prayer, discuss the benefits of praying together as a couple, and provide practical guidance on how to incorporate prayer into daily life. By seeking God's guidance and inviting Him into our relationships through prayer, we can experience a deeper, more enduring love that reflects His divine nature.

The Theological Significance of Prayer in Relationships

Prayer is not just a religious ritual or a means of requesting favors from God; it is a profound expression of our dependence on Him and our desire to align our lives with His will. In relationships, prayer serves as a powerful tool for fostering unity, understanding, and mutual support. It is through prayer that we invite God to be an active participant in our relationships, recognizing that we cannot build and sustain a loving relationship on our own strength.

Theologically, prayer is an acknowledgment of God's sovereignty and wisdom. When we pray, we are admitting that we do not have all the answers and that we need God's guidance and intervention. This humility is essential in relationships, where challenges, conflicts, and uncertainties are inevitable. By turning to God in prayer, we demonstrate our trust in His ability to lead us and to work all things together for our good (Romans 8:28).

Prayer also serves as a means of sanctification in relationships. As we pray, we open our hearts to the transformative work of the Holy Spirit, who molds and shapes us into the image of Christ. This process of sanctification is crucial in relationships, where our flaws, weaknesses, and selfish tendencies can often hinder love and harmony. Through prayer, we invite God to purify our hearts, to remove any barriers to love, and to empower us to love one another as He has loved us.

Moreover, prayer is an expression of our faith in God's promises. In Philippians 4:6-7, Paul encourages believers to bring their concerns to God with thanksgiving, trusting that He will provide peace that surpasses all understanding. This peace is not merely the absence of conflict but a deep, abiding sense of security and contentment that comes from knowing that God is in control. In relationships, this peace is essential, as it allows us to navigate challenges and uncertainties with confidence, knowing that God is with us and that His love is the foundation of our relationship.

The Benefits of Praying Together as a Couple

Praying together as a couple is one of the most powerful ways to strengthen and deepen a relationship. It fosters spiritual intimacy, aligns the couple with God's will, and provides a foundation for mutual support and encouragement. Here are some key benefits of praying together as a couple:

1. Spiritual Intimacy: Prayer is a deeply intimate act that involves sharing one's heart with God and, when done together, with one's partner. When couples pray together, they open themselves up to one another in a way that fosters a deeper connection and understanding. This spiritual intimacy transcends physical and emotional intimacy, creating a bond that is rooted in the shared experience of seeking God's presence and guidance.

2. Unity and Alignment: Praying together helps couples to align their hearts and minds with God's will. It creates a sense of unity, as both partners seek to follow God's leading in their relationship. This unity is crucial in decision-making, conflict resolution, and setting goals for the future. By

praying together, couples can ensure that their relationship is centered on God and that they are working toward the same spiritual goals.

3. Mutual Support and Encouragement: Prayer provides an opportunity for couples to support and encourage one another. When one partner is struggling, the other can lift them up in prayer, offering words of comfort and hope. This mutual support strengthens the relationship and helps both partners to grow in their faith. Additionally, praying for one another fosters a sense of empathy and compassion, as each partner becomes more attuned to the other's needs and concerns.

4. Peace and Security: As mentioned earlier, prayer brings peace that surpasses all understanding (Philippians 4:7). This peace is particularly valuable in relationships, where stress, anxiety, and uncertainty can easily take a toll. When couples pray together, they invite God's peace into their relationship, creating an atmosphere of calm and security. This peace allows couples to face challenges with confidence, knowing that God is in control and that He is working on their behalf.

5. Strengthened Communication: Praying together enhances communication within the relationship. It encourages open and honest dialogue, as couples share their thoughts, feelings, and concerns with God and with each other. This communication fosters a deeper understanding of one another and helps to prevent misunderstandings and miscommunications. Additionally, praying together can help couples to develop a habit of regular, intentional communication, which is essential for a healthy relationship.

6. Spiritual Growth: Praying together is a powerful way to grow spiritually as a couple. It allows both partners to deepen their relationship with God, to learn from one another's faith journey, and to encourage each other in their walk with Christ. This spiritual growth not only strengthens the relationship but also equips the couple to serve God more effectively, both individually and together.

Prayer as a Foundation for a Loving Relationship

A loving relationship is built on a strong foundation of trust, commitment, and mutual respect. Prayer serves as the cornerstone of this foundation, as it connects the couple to God and to one another in a profound and meaningful way. Here are some ways in which prayer can serve as the foundation for a loving relationship:

1. Prayer Cultivates Trust: Trust is essential in any relationship, and prayer helps to cultivate trust by fostering an environment of openness and honesty. When couples pray together, they invite God into their relationship, acknowledging that they are dependent on Him for guidance, wisdom, and strength. This dependence on God fosters trust between partners, as they learn to rely on one another and on God to navigate the challenges of life together.

2. Prayer Strengthens Commitment: Commitment is a key aspect of a loving relationship, and prayer strengthens this commitment by reminding couples of the sacredness of their union. When couples pray together, they reaffirm their commitment to one another and to God, recognizing that their relationship is a covenantal bond that is meant to last a lifetime. This commitment is further reinforced as couples seek God's guidance and wisdom in their relationship, trusting that He will help them to fulfill their vows and to honor their covenant.

3. Prayer Fosters Mutual Respect: Mutual respect is crucial for a healthy and loving relationship, and prayer helps to foster this respect by encouraging couples to see one another through God's eyes. When couples pray together, they are reminded of the inherent worth and dignity of their partner, as a beloved child of God. This perspective fosters a deep sense of respect and appreciation for one another, as couples learn to value each other's thoughts, feelings, and contributions to the relationship.

4. Prayer Encourages Forgiveness: Forgiveness is essential for maintaining a loving relationship, as it allows couples to move past hurt and conflict and to restore their bond. Prayer encourages forgiveness by reminding couples of the forgiveness they have received from God and by empowering them to extend that same forgiveness to one another. When couples pray together, they invite God to heal their hearts, to soften their attitudes, and to help them let go of any resentment or bitterness. This process of forgiveness is crucial for maintaining a healthy and loving relationship, as it fosters reconciliation and renewal.

5. Prayer Builds Emotional Intimacy: Emotional intimacy is a vital component of a loving relationship, and prayer helps to build this intimacy by encouraging couples to share their deepest thoughts, feelings, and desires with one another and with God. This sharing creates a sense of closeness and

connection, as couples learn to support one another emotionally and to bear one another's burdens. Prayer also helps to build emotional intimacy by providing a safe space for couples to express their vulnerabilities and to seek comfort and reassurance from one another.

6. Prayer Enhances Spiritual Intimacy: Spiritual intimacy is the deepest level of connection in a relationship, as it involves a shared commitment to God and a mutual desire to grow in faith together. Prayer enhances spiritual intimacy by fostering a sense of unity and alignment with God's will. When couples pray together, they are united in their pursuit of God's presence, guidance, and purpose for their relationship. This spiritual intimacy not only strengthens the bond between partners but also deepens their relationship with God, creating a strong and enduring foundation for their love.

Practical Guidance for Incorporating Prayer into a Relationship

Incorporating prayer into a relationship requires intentionality and commitment. Here are some practical steps that couples can take to make prayer a regular and meaningful part of their relationship:

1. Establish a Regular Prayer Routine: One of the most effective ways to incorporate prayer into a relationship is to establish a regular prayer routine. This could involve setting aside a specific time each day or week to pray together, whether in the morning, before bed, or during a meal.

Consistency is key, as it helps to build a habit of prayer and to make it a natural part of the relationship.

2. Create a Prayer List: Creating a prayer list can be a helpful way to stay focused and intentional in prayer. Couples can create a list of specific prayer requests, such as personal needs, relationship goals, or concerns for friends and family. This list can be updated regularly and used as a guide during prayer time. Keeping a prayer list also provides an opportunity to celebrate answered prayers and to give thanks for God's faithfulness.

3. Pray for Each Other: Praying for each other is a powerful way to support and encourage one another in the relationship. Couples can take turns praying for each other's needs, concerns, and desires, asking God to bless, guide, and strengthen their partner. Praying for each other also fosters empathy and

compassion, as it helps each partner to understand and appreciate the other's struggles and challenges.

4. Pray Scripture Together: Praying Scripture is a meaningful way to incorporate God's Word into prayer. Couples can choose a passage of Scripture that is relevant to their relationship or a specific situation they are facing and use it as the basis for their prayer. For example, couples can pray through Philippians 4:6-7, asking God to help them overcome anxiety and to fill their relationship with His peace. Praying Scripture helps to align the couple's prayers with God's will and to deepen their understanding of His promises.

5. Pray for Guidance and Wisdom: Seeking God's guidance and wisdom is essential for making decisions in a relationship. Couples can pray together for God's direction in areas such as career choices, financial decisions, or family planning. By seeking God's guidance in prayer, couples demonstrate their trust in His sovereignty and their desire to follow His will for their relationship.

6. Pray for Strength and Endurance: Relationships can be challenging, and there will be times when couples need God's strength and endurance to persevere. Praying for strength and endurance helps couples to rely on God's power rather than their own, trusting that He will sustain them through difficult times. Couples can pray for the courage to face challenges together, the patience to endure trials, and the grace to love one another even when it is difficult.

7. Pray for Protection and Blessing: Couples can pray for God's protection and blessing over their relationship, asking Him to shield them from harm, temptation, and conflict. Praying for protection helps couples to be vigilant against spiritual attacks and to seek God's help in maintaining a healthy and loving relationship. Additionally, couples can pray for God's blessing on their relationship, asking Him to pour out His favor, provision, and joy.

8. Pray with Gratitude: Gratitude is an important aspect of prayer, as it helps to cultivate a positive and thankful attitude. Couples can incorporate gratitude into their prayers by regularly thanking God for the blessings in their relationship, such as the love they share, the growth they experience, and the ways in which God has answered their prayers. Praying with gratitude fosters a sense of contentment and joy, as it reminds couples of God's goodness and faithfulness.

9. Pray for Forgiveness and Healing: Forgiveness is essential for maintaining a loving relationship, and prayer can be a powerful tool for seeking and offering forgiveness. Couples can pray together for God's help in forgiving one another and in healing any wounds or hurts that may exist in the relationship. Praying for forgiveness and healing fosters reconciliation and renewal, allowing couples to move forward in love and unity.

10. Pray for God's Glory: Ultimately, the purpose of prayer in a relationship is to bring glory to God. Couples can pray together for God's glory to be evident in their relationship, asking Him to use their love and commitment as a testimony of His grace and goodness. Praying for God's glory helps couples to keep their relationship centered on Him and to seek His will above all else.

Overcoming Challenges to Praying Together

While praying together as a couple is a powerful way to strengthen a relationship, it can also present challenges. Some couples may struggle with feeling vulnerable or uncomfortable praying together, while others may find it difficult to establish a consistent prayer routine. Here are some common challenges to praying together and practical ways to overcome them:

1. Vulnerability and Fear: Praying together can be a vulnerable experience, as it involves sharing one's heart with both God and one's partner. This vulnerability can be intimidating, especially if one or both partners are not used to praying aloud or sharing their deepest thoughts and feelings. To overcome this challenge, couples can start by praying simple, short prayers together and gradually build up to more in-depth and personal prayers. It's also important to create a safe and non-judgmental environment where both partners feel comfortable expressing themselves.

2. Different Prayer Styles: Couples may have different prayer styles or preferences, which can make it challenging to pray together. For example, one partner may prefer structured prayers, while the other prefers spontaneous, free-flowing prayers. To overcome this challenge, couples can find a balance by incorporating both styles into their prayer time. They can also take turns leading prayer, allowing each partner to pray in their preferred style while also learning from and appreciating the other's approach.

3. Inconsistency and Busyness: Establishing a consistent prayer routine can be difficult, especially in the midst of a busy schedule. Couples may find it challenging to set aside time for prayer, or they may start strong but gradually fall out of the habit. To overcome this challenge, couples can start by setting small, achievable goals, such as praying together for five minutes each day. They can also find creative ways to incorporate prayer into their daily routine, such as praying together during meals, before bed, or during a morning walk.

4. Distractions and Interruptions: Distractions and interruptions can make it difficult to focus during prayer. Whether it's a ringing phone, a noisy environment, or wandering thoughts, distractions can disrupt the flow of prayer and hinder the sense of connection. To overcome this challenge, couples can find a quiet and comfortable place to pray, minimize distractions by turning off electronic devices, and take a few moments to quiet their minds and hearts before beginning prayer.

5. Lack of Confidence: Some individuals may feel insecure or unsure about praying aloud, especially if they are new to prayer or if they feel self-conscious about their words. To overcome this challenge, couples can reassure each other that prayer is not about saying the "right" words but about expressing their hearts to God. They can also practice praying together in a relaxed and informal setting, where there is no pressure to perform or to pray in a specific way.

6. Spiritual Warfare: Prayer is a powerful tool, and the enemy often seeks to hinder it by causing division, doubt, or distraction. Couples may face spiritual attacks that try to disrupt their prayer life or weaken their relationship. To overcome this challenge, couples can pray for protection and strength, recognizing that they are engaged in spiritual warfare and that prayer is their weapon. They can also support and encourage one another in prayer, standing firm in their faith and resisting the enemy's tactics.

Testimonies of the Power of Prayer in Relationships

Throughout history, countless couples have experienced the transformative power of prayer in their relationships. Here are a few testimonies that illustrate the impact of prayer:

1. Reconciliation and Restoration: John and Sarah had been married for ten years when they hit a rough patch in their marriage. They were constantly

arguing, and the love they once shared seemed to have faded. Feeling hopeless, they considered separating. However, a close friend encouraged them to start praying together. At first, it was awkward, but as they persisted, they began to see changes. Through prayer, they found the strength to forgive each other, to communicate more effectively, and to rediscover the love they once had. Today, their marriage is stronger than ever, and they credit the power of prayer for their reconciliation and restoration.

2. Guidance and Direction: Emily and David were faced with a major decision about whether to move to a new city for a job opportunity. They were torn, as the move would require leaving their families and friends behind. Unsure of what to do, they decided to pray together for guidance. Over several weeks, they prayed and sought God's will. Eventually, they both felt a sense of peace and clarity about staying in their current city. Looking back, they see how God guided them through prayer, and they are grateful for the direction they received.

3. Healing and Forgiveness: Maria and Carlos had been married for 15 years when Carlos confessed to having an affair. Maria was devastated and unsure if she could ever forgive him. They separated for a time, but Maria continued to pray for healing and guidance. She felt God leading her to work on forgiveness, and eventually, they began counseling and praying together. Through prayer and God's grace, they were able to rebuild trust and restore their marriage. Today, they share their testimony of healing and forgiveness with other couples, encouraging them to rely on the power of prayer.

4. Strength in Difficult Times: Jessica and Michael faced the heartbreaking loss of their child. The grief was overwhelming, and it put a strain on their relationship. They struggled to find hope and comfort, but they decided to turn to prayer as a way of coping. Praying together allowed them to share their pain with God and with each other. Over time, they found strength in their faith and in their love for one another. Prayer became a source of healing and hope, helping them to navigate the difficult journey of grief.

5. Spiritual Growth: Rachel and Ben had always considered themselves Christians, but it wasn't until they started praying together regularly that they experienced true spiritual growth. Praying together deepened their relationship with God and with each other. They began to see how prayer was transforming their hearts and aligning their lives with God's will. Their marriage became

more joyful and fulfilling as they grew in their faith, and they now see prayer as an essential part of their relationship.

Conclusion

Prayer is a vital component of a loving relationship, serving as the foundation for trust, commitment, and spiritual intimacy. It is through prayer that couples invite God into their relationship, seeking His guidance, wisdom, and strength. By praying together, couples can deepen their connection, align their hearts with God's will, and experience the peace that surpasses all understanding.

As we have seen, prayer plays a crucial role in fostering unity, mutual support, forgiveness, and spiritual growth in relationships. It helps couples to navigate challenges, to build a strong foundation of love and respect, and to grow closer to God and to one another. Whether facing difficult decisions, seeking reconciliation, or simply desiring to draw nearer to God, prayer is the key to a thriving and enduring relationship.

May couples be encouraged to make prayer a regular and integral part of their relationship, trusting in God's promise to hear and answer their prayers. May they experience the transformative power of prayer in their love for one another, and may their relationship be a testament to the goodness and faithfulness of God. As they seek God's guidance and invite Him into their relationship through prayer, may they find the strength, peace, and joy that comes from walking together in His love.

Chapter 8: The Healing Power of Love

Introduction

Love is a powerful force that has the ability to transform lives, restore hope, and heal even the deepest wounds. The Bible speaks profoundly about the healing power of love, particularly in Psalm 147:3, which states, "He heals the brokenhearted and binds up their wounds." This verse beautifully encapsulates the nature of God's love—a love that not only comforts and sustains but also has the power to bring healing and restoration to those who are hurting.

In this chapter, we will explore the concept of love as a healing force, grounded in faith and anchored in the divine love of God. We will reflect on the theological significance of love as a means of healing, examine how love can mend emotional and spiritual wounds, and consider practical ways to cultivate a healing love in our relationships and communities. Through this exploration, we will see how love, when rooted in God's truth and grace, can bring wholeness and peace to broken hearts and lives.

The Theological Foundation of Healing Love

The concept of healing is deeply intertwined with the nature of God's love. Throughout the Bible, God is depicted as a healer—one who mends the brokenhearted, restores the lost, and brings life to those who are spiritually dead. This healing is not just physical but encompasses the whole person, addressing emotional, mental, and spiritual wounds.

In the Old Testament, God reveals Himself as Jehovah-Rapha, "the Lord who heals" (Exodus 15:26). This name reflects God's commitment to the well-being of His people, offering healing not only for their physical ailments but also for their spiritual and emotional wounds. The prophets frequently spoke of God's healing as a sign of His covenantal love, promising restoration and renewal to those who turn to Him in faith.

The New Testament further emphasizes the healing power of love through the ministry of Jesus Christ. Jesus is often portrayed as the ultimate healer, one who brings physical, emotional, and spiritual healing to those in need. His miracles of healing were not just demonstrations of His divine power but also profound acts of love and compassion. In Matthew 9:35-36, we read,

"Jesus went through all the towns and villages, teaching in their synagogues, proclaiming the good news of the kingdom and healing every disease and sickness. When he saw the crowds, he had compassion on them, because they were harassed and helpless, like sheep without a shepherd." Jesus' healing ministry was a tangible expression of God's love, showing that He cares deeply for the broken and the suffering.

Theologically, healing is closely connected to the concept of salvation. The Greek word for salvation, "sozo," can also mean "to heal" or "to make whole." This connection suggests that salvation is not just about being saved from sin but also about being restored to wholeness in every aspect of our being. God's love is the driving force behind this healing, as it seeks to restore us to the fullness of life that He intended for us.

The Healing Power of Love in Emotional Wounds

Emotional wounds are often the most difficult to heal because they penetrate deep into the heart and soul. These wounds can be caused by a variety of experiences, such as betrayal, rejection, loss, abuse, or trauma. They leave scars that can affect our self-esteem, our relationships, and our ability to trust and love others.

The healing power of love is especially potent in addressing emotional wounds. Love, when grounded in faith and expressed with compassion, has the ability to reach into the deepest recesses of our hearts and bring comfort, peace, and restoration. This kind of healing love is patient, kind, and selfless, as described in 1 Corinthians 13:4-7. It does not seek its own advantage but rather seeks to uplift and support the one who is hurting.

One of the most profound examples of the healing power of love in the Bible is the story of the woman with the issue of blood, found in Mark 5:25-34. This woman had suffered from a bleeding condition for twelve years, which not only caused her physical pain but also made her a social outcast. She was considered unclean under Jewish law, and as a result, she was isolated and rejected by her community. Despite her suffering, she believed that if she could just touch the hem of Jesus' garment, she would be healed.

When she finally reached out and touched Jesus, she was instantly healed of her physical condition. But more importantly, Jesus' response to her was an act of profound love. He stopped, acknowledged her, and called her "daughter," affirming her worth and restoring her dignity. Jesus' love not only healed her physically but also addressed the emotional wounds of isolation, rejection, and shame. His love brought her back into the fold of community and gave her a new sense of identity and belonging.

This story illustrates how love, when expressed with compassion and empathy, can heal emotional wounds. Jesus did not just heal the woman's physical ailment; He saw her pain, understood her suffering, and responded with love that restored her whole being. In the same way, when we express love to those who are hurting, we participate in God's healing work, bringing comfort, hope, and restoration to their lives.

The Healing Power of Love in Spiritual Wounds

Spiritual wounds are those that affect our relationship with God and our sense of spiritual well-being. These wounds can be caused by sin, guilt, shame, doubt, or a sense of abandonment by God. They often leave us feeling distant from God, questioning His love, and struggling with feelings of unworthiness.

The healing power of love is particularly important in addressing spiritual wounds, as it helps to restore our relationship with God and to heal the brokenness in our souls. God's love is a healing balm for our spiritual wounds, offering forgiveness, grace, and reconciliation.

One of the most powerful expressions of God's healing love for our spiritual wounds is found in the parable of the prodigal son (Luke 15:11-32). In this parable, a young man demands his inheritance from his father, leaves home, and squanders his wealth in reckless living. Eventually, he finds himself destitute and decides to return home, hoping that his father will take him back as a servant. However, when the father sees his son returning, he runs to him, embraces him, and welcomes him back as a beloved son. The father's love is unconditional and forgiving, offering healing for the son's spiritual wounds of guilt, shame, and estrangement.

The father's love in this parable represents God's love for us. No matter how far we have strayed, God's love is always ready to welcome us back, to forgive us, and to heal our spiritual wounds. His love is not based on our worthiness but on His grace and mercy. When we experience this healing love, we are restored to right relationship with God, and our spiritual wounds are healed.

In addition to God's love, the love of others within the community of faith also plays a crucial role in healing spiritual wounds. When we are struggling with doubt, guilt, or a sense of unworthiness, the love and support of fellow believers can help to restore our faith and renew our sense of connection with God. The church, as the body of Christ, is called to be a place of healing, where love is extended to those who are spiritually wounded, offering them hope, encouragement, and a path to reconciliation with God.

Practical Ways to Cultivate a Healing Love

Cultivating a healing love in our relationships and communities requires intentionality, compassion, and a reliance on God's grace. Here are some practical ways to develop and express a love that brings healing to those who are hurting:

1. Listen with Compassion: One of the most important aspects of healing love is the ability to listen with compassion. When someone is hurting, they often need a safe space to express their pain and to be heard without judgment. Listening with compassion means being fully present, giving the person your undivided attention, and offering empathy and understanding. It involves validating their feelings and acknowledging their pain, without trying to fix or minimize their experience.

2. Offer Words of Affirmation: Words have the power to heal or to harm. Offering words of affirmation can be a powerful way to bring healing to someone who is hurting. This could involve speaking words of encouragement, expressing love and appreciation, or reminding the person of their worth and value in God's eyes. Affirming words can help to counteract the negative messages that may be contributing to the person's emotional or spiritual wounds.

3. Pray for Healing: Prayer is a powerful tool for bringing healing to those who are hurting. Praying for someone who is wounded, whether emotionally or spiritually, invites God's healing presence into their life. It is important to pray not only for physical healing but also for emotional and spiritual healing, asking God to bring peace, comfort, and restoration to the person's heart and

soul. Additionally, praying with the person, if they are open to it, can provide a sense of connection and support, reminding them that they are not alone in their struggle.

4. Extend Forgiveness: Forgiveness is a key component of healing love. When someone has been wounded by another's actions, extending forgiveness can be a powerful step toward healing. This does not mean excusing or condoning the hurtful behavior, but rather choosing to release the person from the debt of their wrongdoing. Forgiveness frees both the forgiver and the forgiven, allowing for healing and restoration to take place. In cases where the wounded person is struggling to forgive themselves, offering reassurance of God's forgiveness and grace can help to facilitate the healing process.

5. Provide Practical Support: Healing love is not just about words; it is also about actions. Providing practical support to someone who is hurting can be a tangible expression of love and care. This could involve helping with daily tasks, offering a listening ear, spending time with the person, or providing resources for counseling or therapy. Practical support demonstrates that you are willing to walk alongside the person in their healing journey and that you care about their well-being.

6. Create a Safe and Supportive Environment: A healing love thrives in an environment that is safe, supportive, and non-judgmental. Creating such an environment involves being intentional about fostering trust, respect, and understanding in your relationships and community. It means being mindful of the words you use, the attitudes you display, and the ways you respond to those who are hurting. A safe and supportive environment allows individuals to be vulnerable, to share their pain, and to seek healing without fear of rejection or judgment.

7. Model Christ's Love: The ultimate model of healing love is found in Jesus Christ. As followers of Christ, we are called to emulate His love in our relationships and interactions with others. This involves showing compassion, extending grace, and being willing to sacrifice for the sake of others. By modeling Christ's love, we become instruments of healing, reflecting His love and grace to those who are hurting.

8. Encourage Connection and Community: Healing often takes place in the context of community. Encouraging those who are hurting to connect with others and to become part of a supportive community can be a powerful

step toward healing. This could involve inviting them to join a small group, encouraging them to attend church, or simply helping them to build meaningful relationships with others. Community provides a sense of belonging, support, and accountability, which are all essential for the healing process.

9. Speak Truth in Love: Healing love involves speaking truth, but it must be done in a loving and compassionate manner. There may be times when it is necessary to address difficult issues or to confront harmful behavior. However, it is important to do so with a heart of love and a desire for the person's healing and restoration. Speaking truth in love means being honest, but also being gentle and respectful, ensuring that your words are motivated by a genuine concern for the person's well-being.

10. Be Patient and Persistent: Healing is often a slow and gradual process, and it requires patience and persistence. It is important to recognize that healing may take time and that the person may go through ups and downs in their journey. Being patient and persistent in your support, even when progress seems slow, demonstrates your commitment to their healing and your belief in the power of love to bring about transformation.

Testimonies of the Healing Power of Love

The healing power of love is not just a theoretical concept; it is a reality that has been experienced by countless individuals throughout history. Here are a few testimonies that illustrate how love, grounded in faith, can heal emotional and spiritual wounds:

1. Healing from Abuse: Sarah had suffered years of emotional and physical abuse at the hands of her partner. The wounds of the abuse left her feeling broken, worthless, and unlovable. However, through the love and support of a close friend who showed her unconditional love and acceptance, Sarah began to experience healing. Her friend's consistent love, combined with counseling and prayer, helped Sarah to rebuild her self-esteem, to forgive her abuser, and to find hope for the future. Today, Sarah is a survivor who uses her story to help others who have experienced similar trauma.

2. Restoration of Faith: David had grown up in a Christian home but had drifted away from his faith during his college years. After experiencing a

series of personal failures and disappointments, he felt distant from God and questioned whether God still loved him. It wasn't until he met a group of believers who welcomed him with open arms and showed him genuine love and acceptance that David began to feel the warmth of God's love again. Through their love and encouragement, David's faith was restored, and he found healing for the spiritual wounds that had kept him distant from God.

3. Healing from Grief: Maria lost her husband to cancer after a long and painful battle. The grief was overwhelming, and she struggled to find a way forward. In the midst of her pain, a group of women from her church surrounded her with love, offering prayers, meals, and companionship. Their love provided a lifeline for Maria, helping her to navigate the dark days of grief and to eventually find hope and healing. While the pain of loss never fully disappeared, Maria found that the love of her friends, combined with her faith in God, helped her to heal and to embrace life once again.

4. Reconciliation and Forgiveness: Tom and Lisa had been married for over 20 years when they experienced a deep rift in their relationship. Hurtful words had been spoken, trust had been broken, and both were carrying wounds that seemed impossible to heal. However, through the intervention of a wise pastor and a commitment to prayer, they were able to begin the process of reconciliation. The pastor's loving guidance, coupled with their willingness to forgive and to seek God's healing, eventually led to the restoration of their marriage. Today, Tom and Lisa share their story with others, testifying to the healing power of love and forgiveness.

5. Healing from Shame: James had carried the weight of shame for many years due to past mistakes and failures. He felt unworthy of love and struggled with feelings of self-condemnation. It wasn't until a mentor in his church began to walk alongside him, offering love, support, and encouragement, that James began to experience healing. His mentor's consistent love, combined with the truth of God's Word, helped James to see himself as God sees him—as forgiven, loved, and redeemed. This healing love transformed James's life, freeing him from the chains of shame and allowing him to live in the fullness of God's grace.

Conclusion

The healing power of love is a testament to the nature of God's love—a love that is compassionate, sacrificial, and redemptive. As we have seen, love, when grounded in faith and expressed with sincerity, has the ability to heal emotional and spiritual wounds, bringing restoration, peace, and wholeness to those who are hurting.

In reflecting on Psalm 147:3, "He heals the brokenhearted and binds up their wounds," we are reminded that God's love is a healing balm for our brokenness. Whether we are dealing with the pain of loss, the wounds of betrayal, the burden of guilt, or the scars of abuse, God's love is sufficient to heal and to restore. His love is not limited by our circumstances or our past; it is a love that reaches into the deepest parts of our hearts and brings healing to our souls.

As we seek to cultivate a healing love in our relationships and communities, may we be inspired by the example of Christ, who demonstrated the ultimate healing love through His life, death, and resurrection. May we be instruments of God's healing love, offering compassion, forgiveness, and support to those who are hurting. And may we always remember that it is through love, grounded in faith, that true healing is found.

In a world that is often marked by pain and brokenness, the healing power of love is a beacon of hope. It is a reminder that no wound is too deep, no heart is too broken, and no soul is too lost for the healing touch of God's love. As we open our hearts to receive this love and as we extend it to others, we participate in God's redemptive work, bringing healing, restoration, and new life to a hurting world.

Chapter 9: Love and Humility
Introduction

Love and humility are two of the most powerful virtues in the Christian faith, and when they are woven together, they create a foundation for deep, meaningful, and enduring relationships. The Apostle Paul, in his letter to the Philippians, offers a profound insight into the connection between love and humility: "Do nothing out of selfish ambition or vain conceit. Rather, in humility value others above yourselves, not looking to your own interests but each of you to the interests of the others" (Philippians 2:3-4). This passage calls believers to a life of humility that is deeply rooted in love—a humility that seeks the well-being of others above one's own desires and fosters relationships marked by mutual respect, care, and selflessness.

In this chapter, we will explore the intricate connection between love and humility, examining how these virtues work together to foster deeper and more meaningful relationships. We will reflect on the theological significance of humility in the context of love, consider the challenges of living out humility in relationships, and provide practical guidance on how to cultivate a humble heart that enhances love. Through this exploration, we will discover that humility is not a sign of weakness, but a powerful expression of love that brings healing, unity, and strength to relationships.

The Theological Foundation of Humility in Love

Humility is a central theme in the teachings of Jesus and is foundational to the Christian understanding of love. In the Gospels, Jesus repeatedly emphasizes the importance of humility, both in His words and in His actions. One of the most striking examples of this is found in John 13, where Jesus, the Son of God, takes on the role of a servant and washes the feet of His disciples. This act of humility is a powerful demonstration of love in action, as Jesus lowers Himself to serve those who follow Him, even though He is their Master and Lord.

Theologically, humility is rooted in the nature of God Himself. Throughout the Bible, God is described as "humble" in the sense that He chooses to draw near to the lowly, the brokenhearted, and the repentant (Isaiah 57:15). This divine humility is most fully revealed in the incarnation of Jesus Christ. In Philippians 2:6-8, Paul writes, "Who, being in very nature God, did not consider equality with God something to be used to his own advantage; rather, he made himself nothing by taking the very nature of a servant, being made in human likeness. And being found in appearance as a man, he humbled himself by becoming obedient to death—even death on a cross!" Jesus' willingness to humble Himself, to take on human flesh, and to suffer and die for the sake of humanity, is the ultimate expression of divine love and humility.

This theological foundation of humility in love challenges the world's understanding of power, status, and relationships. In a culture that often values self-promotion, assertiveness, and individual achievement, the idea of humility—of putting others first and valuing their needs above one's own—can seem counterintuitive or even undesirable. However, in the kingdom of God, humility is a mark of true greatness and a key to building relationships that reflect the self-giving love of Christ.

Humility as an Expression of Love

Humility is essential to the expression of genuine love because it shifts the focus from the self to the other. When we approach relationships with humility, we are better able to see others as they truly are—valuable, worthy of respect, and deserving of love. This perspective allows us to love more deeply, as we seek to serve, honor, and uplift others, rather than seeking to dominate, control, or assert our own interests.

One of the clearest ways that humility expresses itself in love is through selflessness. In Philippians 2:3-4, Paul calls believers to "do nothing out of selfish ambition or vain conceit." Selfish ambition is the opposite of humility; it is the pursuit of one's own desires, status, or recognition at the expense of others. In contrast, humility leads to selflessness—an attitude that prioritizes the needs and well-being of others above one's own. This selflessness is a reflection of the love of Christ, who "did not come to be served, but to serve, and to give his life as a ransom for many" (Matthew 20:28).

Humility also expresses itself in love through empathy and compassion. When we are humble, we are more attuned to the feelings, struggles, and experiences of others. We are willing to step into their shoes, to see the world from their perspective, and to respond with kindness and understanding. This empathy fosters deeper connections and helps to build trust and intimacy in relationships. It also allows us to be more patient, forgiving, and supportive, as we recognize that we too have our own flaws and weaknesses.

Furthermore, humility in love is expressed through the willingness to serve. Jesus' act of washing His disciples' feet is a powerful example of how humility leads to service. In relationships, humility motivates us to serve others, not out of obligation or a desire for recognition, but out of genuine love and concern for their well-being. This service can take many forms—listening attentively, offering help, sacrificing time or resources, or simply being present with someone in their time of need. When we serve others with humility, we demonstrate the love of Christ and reflect His character to the world.

The Challenges of Living Out Humility in Relationships

While humility is essential for building deep and meaningful relationships, it is not always easy to practice. There are several challenges that can make it difficult to live out humility in our interactions with others, particularly in a culture that often values self-assertion and individualism.

1. Pride and Ego: One of the greatest obstacles to humility is pride. Pride is the opposite of humility; it is an inflated sense of self-importance and a desire for recognition, power, and control. Pride can manifest in many ways—through arrogance, defensiveness, stubbornness, or a refusal to admit mistakes. In relationships, pride can create barriers to intimacy, trust, and communication, as it often leads to conflicts, misunderstandings, and a lack of willingness to compromise or listen to others.

2. Fear of Vulnerability: Humility often requires us to be vulnerable, to admit our weaknesses, to ask for help, or to put the needs of others above our own. This vulnerability can be frightening, especially in a world that often equates vulnerability with weakness. The fear of being taken advantage of, judged, or rejected can make it difficult to practice humility, leading us to protect our pride and to prioritize our own interests over the well-being of others.

3. Cultural Pressures: We live in a culture that frequently promotes self-promotion, competition, and individual achievement. The pressure to succeed, to stand out, and to assert oneself can make it challenging to embrace humility. This cultural mindset can also influence our relationships, leading us

to approach interactions with a transactional or competitive mindset, rather than a spirit of humility and service.

4. Misunderstandings of Humility: Humility is sometimes misunderstood as passivity, low self-esteem, or a lack of confidence. These misconceptions can make it difficult to embrace humility, as people may fear that being humble means being weak, ineffective, or unassertive. However, true humility is not about diminishing oneself; it is about recognizing one's worth in God's eyes while also valuing and honoring others.

5. The Desire for Control: In relationships, the desire for control can be a significant barrier to humility. Whether it is controlling the outcome of a situation, controlling how others perceive us, or controlling the dynamics of a relationship, the need for control often stems from a lack of trust and a fear of uncertainty. This desire for control can lead to manipulation, defensiveness, and a lack of openness, all of which hinder the development of deep and meaningful relationships.

Cultivating Humility in Love

Cultivating humility in our relationships requires intentional effort, self-reflection, and a reliance on God's grace. Here are some practical ways to develop and practice humility in love:

1. Practice Self-Examination: Regular self-examination is essential for cultivating humility. Take time to reflect on your thoughts, attitudes, and behaviors in your relationships. Ask yourself whether you are motivated by love and selflessness, or by pride and selfish ambition. Be honest about your weaknesses and areas where you struggle with humility. This self-awareness is the first step toward growth and transformation.

2. Seek God's Help: Humility is a fruit of the Holy Spirit, and we cannot cultivate it on our own. Pray for God's help in developing a humble heart. Ask Him to reveal areas where pride may be hindering your relationships, and to give you the grace to respond with humility and love. Surrender your need for control, recognition, and self-importance to God, trusting that He will guide you in the path of humility.

3. Focus on Others: One of the most effective ways to practice humility is to focus on the needs, feelings, and well-being of others. Make a conscious

effort to listen attentively, to empathize with others, and to prioritize their interests above your own. This might involve small acts of kindness, such as offering a word of encouragement, helping someone in need, or simply being present with someone who is going through a difficult time.

4. Embrace Vulnerability: Humility often requires us to be vulnerable, to admit our weaknesses, to ask for help, or to let go of our need for control. Embrace this vulnerability as an opportunity to grow in humility and to deepen your relationships. Recognize that vulnerability is not a sign of weakness, but a strength that allows you to connect more authentically with others.

5. Be Open to Feedback: Being open to feedback is an important aspect of humility. Instead of becoming defensive or dismissive when someone offers constructive criticism, take it as an opportunity to learn and grow. Acknowledge that you are not perfect, and be willing to consider how you can improve in your relationships. This openness to feedback demonstrates a humble and teachable spirit.

6. Apologize and Forgive Humility involves recognizing when you have wronged someone and being willing to apologize. A sincere apology requires humility, as it involves admitting your mistakes and seeking reconciliation. Similarly, humility is necessary for forgiveness, as it involves letting go of pride, resentment, and the desire for revenge. Cultivate a heart that is quick to apologize and quick to forgive, recognizing that these actions are expressions of love and humility.

7. Serve Others: Serving others is one of the most tangible expressions of humility. Look for opportunities to serve those around you, whether it is within your family, your community, or your church. Serving others involves putting their needs above your own and being willing to sacrifice your time, energy, and resources for their benefit. This act of service not only blesses others but also helps to cultivate a humble and selfless heart.

8. Meditate on Christ's Example : The ultimate example of humility is found in Jesus Christ. Take time to meditate on the life and teachings of Jesus, particularly His humility in serving others and His willingness to lay down His life for the sake of humanity. Reflecting on Christ's example can inspire and motivate you to cultivate humility in your own life. As you meditate on His humility, ask God to help you embody this same humility in your relationships.

9. Cultivate Gratitude: Gratitude is closely linked to humility, as it involves recognizing that all good things come from God and that we are dependent on His grace. Cultivate a spirit of gratitude by regularly thanking God for His blessings, acknowledging the contributions of others, and appreciating the love and support you receive from those around you. Gratitude helps to shift the focus from yourself to others, fostering a heart of humility.

10. Practice Patience and Gentleness: Humility is often expressed through patience and gentleness in relationships. Practice being patient with others, especially when they make mistakes or fall short of your expectations. Respond with gentleness, rather than harshness or judgment. This patience and gentleness are reflections of a humble heart that seeks to love and uplift others, rather than to assert power or control.

The Impact of Humility on Relationships

When humility is practiced in relationships, it has a profound impact on the quality and depth of those connections. Humility fosters an environment of trust, respect, and mutual care, creating the conditions for healthy and meaningful relationships to flourish.

1. Deepening of Intimacy: Humility allows for greater intimacy in relationships, as it fosters open and honest communication, empathy, and understanding. When both parties are willing to be vulnerable, to admit their weaknesses, and to prioritize the well-being of the other, the relationship becomes more authentic and deeply connected. This intimacy is not just emotional, but also spiritual, as humility opens the door for mutual growth and encouragement in the faith.

2. Resolution of Conflicts: Humility plays a crucial role in resolving conflicts in relationships. When both parties approach a conflict with humility, they are more likely to listen to each other's perspectives, to acknowledge their own faults, and to seek reconciliation. Humility helps to de-escalate tensions, to find common ground, and to work toward a solution that honors both parties. It also makes it easier to forgive and to move past the hurt, as humility fosters a spirit of grace and understanding.

3. Strengthening of Trust: Trust is a cornerstone of any healthy relationship, and humility is essential for building and maintaining trust.

When someone consistently demonstrates humility—by being honest, reliable, and selfless—trust naturally grows. Humility also makes it easier to repair trust when it has been broken, as it involves acknowledging mistakes, seeking forgiveness, and making amends. A relationship built on humility is one where both parties feel safe, respected, and valued.

4. Fostering of Mutual Respect: Humility fosters mutual respect in relationships, as it involves recognizing the worth and dignity of the other person. When we approach relationships with humility, we are more likely to honor the opinions, feelings, and contributions of others. This mutual respect creates a healthy dynamic in the relationship, where both parties feel valued and appreciated. It also helps to prevent power imbalances, as humility encourages equality and collaboration.

5. Promotion of Growth and Learning: Relationships that are characterized by humility are conducive to growth and learning. Humility involves a willingness to learn from others, to accept feedback, and to grow in response to challenges. In a humble relationship, both parties are open to personal and relational growth, which leads to a deeper and more fulfilling connection. This growth is not just individual but also collective, as the relationship itself becomes stronger and more resilient over time.

6. Creation of a Loving and Supportive Environment: Humility creates a loving and supportive environment in relationships, where both parties feel safe to be themselves and to share their struggles. In such an environment, there is less fear of judgment or rejection, as both parties are committed to loving and supporting each other unconditionally. This loving environment fosters a sense of belonging, security, and joy, making the relationship a source of comfort and encouragement.

Testimonies of the Power of Humility in Love

Throughout history, countless individuals have experienced the transformative power of humility in their relationships. Here are a few testimonies that illustrate how humility can deepen love and foster meaningful connections:

1. Reconciliation After a Rift: Tom and Sarah had been married for several years when they experienced a deep rift in their relationship. Hurtful words were exchanged, and both were unwilling to back down or admit their faults.

The tension escalated, leading to a period of separation. However, after seeking counsel from a trusted mentor, Tom decided to approach Sarah with humility. He apologized for his part in the conflict and expressed a genuine desire to reconcile. Sarah, seeing his humility, softened her heart and admitted her own faults as well. Together, they worked through their issues and restored their relationship. Today, they credit the power of humility for saving their marriage and bringing them closer together.

2. Healing of a Broken Friendship: Jane and Emily had been close friends for years when a misunderstanding led to a falling out. Both felt hurt and betrayed, and neither was willing to make the first move toward reconciliation. However, after praying for guidance, Jane felt convicted to approach Emily with humility. She acknowledged her role in the conflict and asked for forgiveness. Emily, moved by Jane's humility, also admitted her mistakes and expressed her desire to restore the friendship. Through humility, their friendship was healed, and they grew even closer as a result.

3. Transformation of a Family Dynamic: Michael grew up in a family where pride and competition were prevalent. As an adult, he realized that these dynamics were causing tension and distance between family members. Determined to change the dynamic, Michael began to practice humility in his interactions with his family. He stopped trying to prove himself, listened more, and made an effort to serve and support his family members. Over time, his humility began to influence others in the family, leading to more open communication, mutual respect, and a stronger sense of unity. Today, Michael's family enjoys a healthier and more loving relationship, thanks to the power of humility.

4. Strengthening of a Marriage: Lisa and John had a good marriage, but they often struggled with communication and misunderstandings. John tended to be more assertive, while Lisa was more reserved, leading to a power imbalance in their relationship. After attending a marriage retreat, John realized that his assertiveness was rooted in pride and a desire for control. He committed to practicing humility in his marriage by listening more, being patient, and valuing Lisa's opinions. As John embraced humility, Lisa felt more confident and respected, leading to better communication and a stronger, more balanced marriage.

5. Restoration of a Parent-Child Relationship: Susan had a strained relationship with her adult daughter, Amy, due to years of misunderstandings and unmet expectations. Both felt hurt and distant, and their interactions were often tense. After a period of reflection, Susan realized that she had been too controlling and critical of Amy. She decided to approach Amy with humility, expressing her regret for her past behavior and asking for forgiveness. Amy, touched by her mother's humility, opened up about her own feelings and expressed a desire to rebuild their relationship. Through humility, their relationship was restored, and they now enjoy a closer bond.

Conclusion

Love and humility are inseparable virtues that, when practiced together, have the power to transform relationships. As we have seen, humility is not a sign of weakness, but a powerful expression of love that fosters trust, respect, intimacy, and mutual growth. It challenges the world's values of pride, self-promotion, and control, offering instead a path of selflessness, service, and vulnerability.

In reflecting on Philippians 2:3-4, we are reminded that humility involves valuing others above ourselves and looking to their interests with love and care. This humility, modeled after Christ's own example, is the key to building deep and meaningful relationships that reflect the self-giving love of God.

As we seek to cultivate humility in our relationships, may we be inspired by the example of Christ, who humbled Himself for our sake and demonstrated the ultimate expression of love. May we practice humility with intentionality, relying on God's grace to transform our hearts and to guide us in our interactions with others. And may our relationships be marked by the beauty of humility, as we seek to love, serve, and honor one another in the spirit of Christ.

In a world that often elevates pride and self-importance, the practice of humility stands as a powerful testimony to the transformative power of love. As we embrace humility in our relationships, we participate in God's redemptive work, bringing healing, unity, and strength to a world in need of His love.

Chapter 10: The Joy of Love

Introduction

Joy is a profound and powerful emotion, one that is often sought after but can be elusive in a world filled with challenges and hardships. In the Christian faith, joy is more than just a fleeting feeling; it is a deep, abiding state of contentment and gladness that comes from a relationship with God. This joy, rooted in divine love, has the power to sustain and enrich human relationships in ways that go beyond mere happiness or pleasure. In Nehemiah 8:10, we find the declaration, "The joy of the Lord is your strength." This verse encapsulates the idea that true joy, which comes from God, is a source of strength and vitality in our lives, particularly in our relationships.

In this chapter, we will explore the concept of the joy of love, reflecting on how divine love brings joy into our lives and how this joy can be the foundation for strong, meaningful, and enduring relationships. We will delve into the theological significance of joy, examine the ways in which joy enriches human connections, and provide practical guidance on how to cultivate and sustain joy in our relationships. Through this exploration, we will discover that joy, when rooted in love, is not only a source of personal fulfillment but also a powerful force that can transform our relationships and our communities.

The Theological Foundation of Joy in Divine Love

Joy, in the Christian context, is deeply intertwined with the concept of divine love. It is a joy that is not dependent on external circumstances but is rooted in the unchanging nature of God's love for us. Throughout the Bible, joy is frequently mentioned as a fruit of the Spirit and a hallmark of the Christian life. This joy is not merely an emotional response to positive events but a deep-seated assurance that comes from knowing and experiencing God's love.

Theologically, joy is seen as a reflection of God's character. In the Old Testament, joy is often associated with God's presence and His acts of salvation. For example, in the Psalms, we read, "In your presence there is fullness of joy; at your right hand are pleasures forevermore" (Psalm 16:11). This verse highlights the idea that true joy is found in the presence of God, where His love and goodness are fully experienced.

In the New Testament, joy is closely linked to the Gospel—the good news of Jesus Christ. The angel who announced the birth of Jesus declared, "I bring you good news that will cause great joy for all the people" (Luke 2:10). This joy stems from the realization that through Christ, we are reconciled to God, forgiven of our sins, and given the promise of eternal life. It is a joy that transcends earthly troubles and is rooted in the hope and assurance of God's love and salvation.

The Apostle Paul further emphasizes the connection between joy and love in his letter to the Philippians. Despite being in prison, Paul writes, "Rejoice in the Lord always. I will say it again: Rejoice!" (Philippians 4:4). Paul's joy is not based on his circumstances but on his relationship with Christ and the love that he has experienced through the Gospel. This joy is a testimony to the power of divine love to bring contentment and gladness even in the midst of trials.

In essence, the joy that comes from divine love is a gift from God, one that sustains us through life's challenges and enriches our relationships. It is a joy that is rooted in the knowledge that we are loved unconditionally by God, that we are His children, and that nothing can separate us from His love (Romans 8:38-39). This joy is a wellspring of strength, enabling us to love others more fully and to build relationships that are marked by grace, patience, and enduring love.

The Joy of Love in Human Relationships

The joy that stems from divine love has a profound impact on human relationships. When our hearts are filled with the joy of the Lord, it overflows into our interactions with others, enriching and deepening our connections. This joy brings vitality to relationships, fostering a sense of fulfillment, contentment, and mutual respect. Here are some ways in which the joy of love manifests in human relationships:

1. Joy as a Source of Strength: As Nehemiah 8:10 declares, "The joy of the Lord is your strength." In relationships, this joy provides the strength to endure difficult times, to overcome challenges, and to remain committed to one another. Whether in marriage, friendship, or family relationships, the joy that comes from God's love helps us to persevere, to forgive, and to continue loving even when it is difficult. This strength is not born out of sheer willpower but is

rooted in the joy that comes from knowing that we are loved by God and that His love empowers us to love others.

2. Joy as a Catalyst for Gratitude: Joy and gratitude are closely connected. When we experience the joy of the Lord, it naturally leads to a sense of gratitude for the blessings in our lives, including our relationships. This gratitude fosters a positive and appreciative attitude toward others, helping us to focus on their strengths and the good that they bring into our lives, rather than on their shortcomings or the challenges we may face. Gratitude, in turn, strengthens relationships by creating an atmosphere of appreciation, respect, and mutual encouragement.

3. Joy as a Foundation for Contentment: In a world that often promotes discontentment and the constant pursuit of more, the joy of the Lord brings a sense of contentment that is not dependent on external circumstances. This contentment allows us to be satisfied with the relationships we have, to appreciate the people in our lives, and to avoid the pitfalls of envy, comparison, or dissatisfaction. Contentment rooted in joy helps us to focus on nurturing and building our relationships, rather than constantly seeking something new or better.

4. Joy as an Antidote to Fear and Worry: Fear and worry can be significant obstacles to healthy relationships. Whether it is the fear of losing someone, the fear of being hurt, or the worry about the future, these emotions can create distance and tension in relationships. The joy of the Lord, however, is a powerful antidote to fear and worry. As Paul writes in Philippians 4:6-7, "Do not be anxious about anything, but in every situation, by prayer and petition, with thanksgiving, present your requests to God. And the peace of God, which transcends all understanding, will guard your hearts and your minds in Christ Jesus." This peace, which is closely related to joy, helps to calm our fears and to trust in God's love and providence, allowing us to engage more fully and openly in our relationships.

5. Joy as a Source of Generosity: Joyful hearts are generous hearts. When we are filled with the joy of the Lord, we are more inclined to give of ourselves—our time, our resources, our love—to others. This generosity is not motivated by a sense of obligation or duty, but by the overflowing joy that comes from experiencing God's love. Generosity, in turn, enriches relationships by fostering a spirit of selflessness, kindness, and mutual care. It helps to build

trust and deepen connections, as we invest in the well-being and happiness of those we love.

6. Joy as a Means of Building Resilience: Relationships are not without their challenges, and there will be times when misunderstandings, conflicts, or external pressures threaten to weaken the bonds we share. The joy of the Lord, however, provides the resilience needed to navigate these challenges. It gives us the perspective to see beyond the immediate difficulties and to focus on the long-term health and growth of the relationship. Joy enables us to approach conflicts with a spirit of reconciliation and grace, rather than with anger or defensiveness. This resilience helps to strengthen relationships over time, as we learn to work through challenges together with patience and love.

7. Joy as a Source of Delight in Others: The joy of the Lord enables us to delight in the people we love. This delight is not based on their perfection or on what they can do for us, but on the simple fact that they are precious to us and to God. When we delight in others, we are more likely to express our love and appreciation, to celebrate their successes, and to support them in their struggles. This delight fosters a sense of joy and fulfillment in the relationship, creating a positive and uplifting atmosphere.

8. Joy as a Reflection of God's Love: Ultimately, the joy of love in relationships is a reflection of God's love for us. When we experience the joy of the Lord, it is a reminder that we are loved deeply and unconditionally by God. This realization allows us to love others more freely and fully, as we are no longer seeking to fill a void or to earn love through our relationships. Instead, we can give and receive love with joy, knowing that our identity and worth are secure in God's love.

Cultivating the Joy of Love in Relationships

Cultivating the joy of love in relationships requires intentional effort, a focus on spiritual growth, and a commitment to nurturing and enriching our connections with others. Here are some practical ways to cultivate and sustain the joy of love in your relationships:

1. Nurture Your Relationship with God: The joy of the Lord is the foundation for joy in all other areas of life, including relationships. To cultivate this joy, it is essential to nurture your relationship with God through prayer,

worship, and the study of His Word. As you grow in your relationship with God, His love will fill your heart with joy, which will naturally overflow into your interactions with others. Make time for regular spiritual practices that help you to connect with God and to experience His presence and love.

2. Practice Gratitude Daily**: Gratitude is a powerful way to cultivate joy in your relationships. Make it a habit to express gratitude for the people in your life and the ways in which they bless and enrich your life. This could involve keeping a gratitude journal, where you write down specific things you are thankful for each day, or simply taking a moment each day to thank God for the relationships He has given you. Expressing gratitude to the people in your life is also important—let them know how much you appreciate them and the joy they bring into your life.

3. Celebrate the Goodness in Others: One of the best ways to cultivate joy in relationships is to celebrate the goodness in others. Focus on their positive qualities, their strengths, and the contributions they make to your life and the lives of others. Take the time to acknowledge and affirm these qualities, both to yourself and to them. Celebrating others in this way fosters a sense of joy and appreciation, and it strengthens the bonds of love and respect in the relationship.

4. Invest in the Well-Being of Others: Joy in relationships is often cultivated through acts of love and service. Invest in the well-being of the people you love by being attentive to their needs, offering support, and showing kindness and generosity. This could involve simple acts of service, such as helping with household tasks, offering a listening ear, or spending quality time together. When we invest in the well-being of others, we not only bring joy to their lives but also experience a deep sense of fulfillment and joy ourselves.

5. Cultivate a Spirit of Contentment: Contentment is closely linked to joy, as it involves being satisfied with what we have and who we are, rather than constantly seeking more. Cultivate a spirit of contentment in your relationships by focusing on the present moment and appreciating the people in your life as they are, without wishing for something different or better. Contentment helps to reduce feelings of envy, comparison, or dissatisfaction, and it allows you to fully enjoy and cherish your relationships.

6. Choose Joy in Difficult Times: There will be times when joy is hard to find, particularly in the midst of challenges or conflicts in relationships.

However, choosing joy is a deliberate act of faith, one that involves trusting in God's goodness and love even in difficult circumstances. In these times, focus on the blessings that remain, the lessons that can be learned, and the ways in which God is at work in your life and relationships. Choosing joy in difficult times helps to build resilience and to strengthen your relationships, as it allows you to navigate challenges with grace and hope.

7. Engage in Joyful Activities Together: Joy can be cultivated through shared experiences and activities that bring happiness and fulfillment to both you and the people you love. Engage in activities that you both enjoy, whether it's going for a walk, playing a game, cooking a meal together, or simply spending time talking and laughing. These joyful activities create positive memories and strengthen the bond between you, fostering a sense of joy and connection in the relationship.

8. Be Present in the Moment: One of the keys to experiencing joy in relationships is being fully present in the moment. This means putting aside distractions, such as phones or worries, and focusing on the person you are with. Being present allows you to fully engage with the other person, to listen attentively, and to appreciate the time you have together. When we are present in the moment, we are more likely to experience the joy of love in our relationships.

9. Pray for Joy in Your Relationships: Prayer is a powerful way to invite God's joy into your relationships. Pray for the people you love, asking God to fill their hearts with His joy and to bless your relationship with a deep sense of contentment and fulfillment. Pray for the strength to choose joy, even in difficult times, and for the wisdom to cultivate joy in your interactions with others. Trust that God, who is the source of all joy, will answer your prayers and will work in your relationships to bring about His good purposes.

10. Reflect on the Joy of God's Love: Finally, take time to reflect on the joy that comes from knowing and experiencing God's love. Meditate on the ways in which God's love has brought joy and fulfillment into your life, and let this joy be the foundation for how you love and interact with others. As you reflect on God's love, allow it to fill your heart with gratitude, contentment, and a deep sense of joy that sustains and enriches your relationships.

The Impact of Joyful Love on Relationships

When joy, rooted in divine love, is cultivated in relationships, it has a transformative impact. Joyful love brings vitality, resilience, and depth to relationships, creating an environment where love can flourish and grow. Here are some of the ways in which joyful love impacts relationships:

1. Strengthening of Bonds: Joyful love strengthens the bonds between individuals by fostering a sense of connection, trust, and mutual respect. When relationships are characterized by joy, they become a source of comfort, support, and encouragement, where both parties feel valued and appreciated. This strengthens the foundation of the relationship, making it more resilient to challenges and conflicts.

2. Enhancement of Communication: Joyful love enhances communication in relationships by creating an atmosphere of openness and positivity. When both parties are filled with joy, they are more likely to communicate with kindness, patience, and understanding. This leads to more effective and meaningful conversations, where both parties feel heard and respected. Joyful communication also helps to prevent misunderstandings and to resolve conflicts in a constructive and loving manner.

3. Increase in Mutual Support: Relationships characterized by joyful love are marked by a high level of mutual support and care. When we experience joy in our relationships, we are more inclined to support and encourage one another, to celebrate each other's successes, and to stand by each other in difficult times. This mutual support strengthens the relationship and helps both parties to grow and thrive together.

4. Fostering of a Positive Environment: Joyful love creates a positive environment in relationships, where both parties feel safe, accepted, and loved. This positive environment fosters a sense of security and well-being, allowing both parties to be themselves and to share their thoughts, feelings, and experiences openly. A positive environment also encourages growth, creativity, and the pursuit of shared goals and dreams, making the relationship a source of fulfillment and joy.

5. Encouragement of Growth and Development Joyful love encourages growth and development in relationships, as it creates a supportive and nurturing environment where both parties can flourish. When relationships

are characterized by joy, both parties are more likely to pursue personal and relational growth, to take on new challenges, and to support each other in their individual and shared goals. This growth leads to a deeper and more fulfilling relationship, where both parties continue to evolve and grow together.

6. Promotion of Long-Term Commitment: Joyful love promotes long-term commitment in relationships by fostering a deep sense of contentment, fulfillment, and satisfaction. When both parties experience joy in their relationship, they are more likely to remain committed to each other, to work through challenges together, and to invest in the long-term health and well-being of the relationship. This commitment is not based on obligation or duty, but on the joy that comes from being in a loving and supportive relationship.

7. Creation of a Legacy of Love: Relationships characterized by joyful love leave a lasting legacy of love, not only for the individuals involved but also for those around them. Joyful relationships serve as a testimony to the power of God's love to transform and enrich human connections. They inspire others to pursue joyful and loving relationships, to prioritize love and connection, and to seek the joy that comes from a relationship with God. This legacy of love has a ripple effect, influencing families, communities, and future generations.

Testimonies of the Joy of Love in Relationships

The joy of love is not just a concept; it is a lived experience that has brought fulfillment and transformation to countless individuals and relationships. Here are a few testimonies that illustrate the impact of joyful love on relationships:

1. Renewal of Marital Joy: Karen and Mark had been married for over 20 years when they realized that the joy in their marriage had faded. The stresses of work, raising children, and dealing with life's challenges had taken a toll on their relationship. Determined to rekindle the joy in their marriage, they began to pray together, to express gratitude for each other daily, and to engage in activities that they both enjoyed. Over time, they began to experience a renewed sense of joy and fulfillment in their marriage. Today, they are closer than ever, and they credit the joy of the Lord for revitalizing their relationship.

2. Finding Joy in Friendship: Emily and Sarah had been friends since childhood, but as they grew older, their lives took different paths, and they

began to drift apart. Both felt the loss of their close friendship but were unsure how to reconnect. After a mutual friend suggested they attend a retreat together, they decided to give it a try. During the retreat, they reconnected and realized how much joy their friendship had brought to their lives. They committed to making time for each other and to nurturing their friendship with intentionality. Today, their friendship is a source of joy, support, and encouragement, and they are grateful for the gift of joyful love in their relationship.

3. Joy in Parenting: John and Lisa struggled with the challenges of raising their two children, especially during the teenage years. The stresses of parenting often overshadowed the joy they had once felt. After attending a parenting workshop at their church, they learned about the importance of cultivating joy in their relationship with their children. They began to focus on the positive aspects of their children's personalities, to express their love and appreciation more openly, and to create joyful family traditions. As a result, their relationship with their children improved, and they began to experience the joy of parenting once again.

4. Joy in Serving Others: David and Mary had always been involved in their community, but they often felt that their efforts were met with indifference or unappreciation. This led to feelings of burnout and frustration. However, after attending a sermon on the joy of serving others, they realized that their motivation for service needed to be rooted in the joy of the Lord, rather than in seeking recognition or approval from others. They recommitted themselves to serving with joy and found that their efforts were more fulfilling and impactful. Today, they continue to serve their community with joy, knowing that they are making a difference through the love of Christ.

5. Joy in Reconciliation: Jane and Tom had experienced a falling out that led to years of estrangement. Both longed for reconciliation but were unsure how to bridge the gap. After attending a healing service at their church, they felt prompted to reach out to each other. They met, prayed together, and asked for forgiveness. As they reconciled, they were overwhelmed by the joy of being reunited. Their relationship was restored, and they continue to experience the joy of love in their renewed connection.

Conclusion

The joy of love is a gift from God, one that has the power to sustain and enrich our relationships in ways that go beyond mere happiness or satisfaction. As we have seen, joy, when rooted in divine love, provides strength, contentment, and resilience in our relationships. It fosters a spirit of gratitude, generosity, and delight, creating an environment where love can flourish and grow.

In reflecting on Nehemiah 8:10, "The joy of the Lord is your strength," we are reminded that true joy comes from a relationship with God and that this joy is a source of strength in all aspects of our lives, including our relationships. When we cultivate the joy of the Lord in our hearts, it naturally overflows into our interactions with others, enriching and deepening our connections.

As we seek to cultivate the joy of love in our relationships, may we be inspired by the example of Christ, who embodied the joy of divine love in His life and ministry. May we practice gratitude, contentment, and generosity in our relationships, and may we choose joy even in difficult times, trusting that God's love is sufficient to sustain us.

In a world that often seeks joy in temporary pleasures or external circumstances, the joy of love stands as a powerful testimony to the enduring and transformative power of God's love. As we embrace this joy in our relationships, we participate in God's redemptive work, bringing light, hope, and love to a world in need of His joy.

Chapter 11: Overcoming Fear with Love

Introduction

Fear is a powerful and pervasive emotion, one that can influence our thoughts, behaviors, and relationships in profound ways. Whether it's the fear of rejection, failure, loss, or vulnerability, fear has the potential to create barriers that prevent us from fully experiencing love and intimacy in our relationships. However, the Bible offers a powerful antidote to fear: love. In 1 John 4:18, we find the profound truth that "There is no fear in love. But perfect love drives out fear, because fear has to do with punishment. The one who fears is not made perfect in love." This verse highlights the transformative power of love to overcome fear, fostering trust, openness, and deeper connections in our relationships.

In this chapter, we will explore the concept of overcoming fear with love, reflecting on how perfect love casts out fear and creates a foundation for trust and openness in relationships. We will delve into the theological significance of love as the antidote to fear, examine the various forms of fear that can impact relationships, and provide practical guidance on how to cultivate love that overcomes fear. Through this exploration, we will discover that love, when rooted in God's truth and grace, has the power to break down the walls of fear and to build relationships that are marked by trust, authenticity, and deep connection.

The Theological Foundation of Love as the Antidote to Fear

The Bible consistently presents love as the most powerful force in the universe, one that originates from God and is capable of transforming lives, relationships, and even the world. In 1 John 4:7-8, we read, "Dear friends, let us love one another, for love comes from God. Everyone who loves has been born of God and knows God. Whoever does not love does not know God, because God is love." This passage underscores the idea that love is not just an emotion or a feeling; it is the very nature and essence of God. Therefore, when we experience and express love, we are participating in the divine nature and reflecting the character of God.

Fear, on the other hand, is often associated with the brokenness of the human condition. It is a byproduct of the fall, where humanity's separation from God introduced insecurity, anxiety, and the fear of punishment. In the Garden of Eden, Adam and Eve's disobedience led to the first experience of fear, as they hid from God, ashamed and afraid of His judgment (Genesis 3:8-10). This fear of judgment and separation has continued to plague humanity throughout history, manifesting in various forms in our lives and relationships.

Theologically, love is presented as the ultimate antidote to fear because it is rooted in the very character of God, who is love. In 1 John 4:18, the apostle John makes a profound connection between love and fear: "There is no fear in love. But perfect love drives out fear, because fear has to do with punishment. The one who fears is not made perfect in love." This verse reveals that fear is incompatible with perfect love because fear is rooted in the anticipation of punishment, rejection, or harm. However, when we are filled with the love of God—a love that is unconditional, sacrificial, and steadfast—there is no room for fear. This love casts out fear by assuring us of our security in God's love, our worth in His eyes, and our acceptance as His beloved children.

The concept of "perfect love" in this verse is crucial. Perfect love does not mean flawless love on our part, but rather the complete and mature love that comes from God. It is a love that is perfected in us as we grow in our relationship with God and as we learn to love others as He loves us. This love is characterized by selflessness, sacrifice, and a deep concern for the well-being of others. As we are filled with this perfect love, fear loses its grip on our hearts, and we are free to engage in relationships with trust, openness, and vulnerability.

Understanding the Various Forms of Fear in Relationships

Fear can manifest in many different forms in relationships, and it often creates barriers that prevent us from fully experiencing love and intimacy. Some of the most common forms of fear that impact relationships include:

1. Fear of Rejection: The fear of rejection is one of the most pervasive fears in relationships. It is the fear that others will not accept us, love us, or want to be in a relationship with us if they truly know who we are. This fear often leads to self-protective behaviors, such as putting up walls, hiding our true selves, or

avoiding vulnerability. The fear of rejection can prevent us from forming deep and meaningful connections, as we are constantly worried about being rejected or abandoned.

2. Fear of Vulnerability: Vulnerability is an essential component of intimacy in relationships, but it also requires a willingness to be open and exposed, which can be frightening. The fear of vulnerability is the fear of being hurt, judged, or taken advantage of if we reveal our true selves or share our deepest thoughts and feelings. This fear often leads to emotional distance, a reluctance to open up, and a tendency to keep others at arm's length.

3. Fear of Failure: The fear of failure in relationships is the fear that we will not be able to meet the expectations of others or that we will somehow fall short in our role as a partner, friend, or family member. This fear can lead to perfectionism, people-pleasing behaviors, or a reluctance to take risks in the relationship. The fear of failure can also create a sense of inadequacy and insecurity, which can undermine the foundation of trust and confidence in the relationship.

4. Fear of Loss: The fear of loss is the fear that we will lose someone we love, whether through death, separation, or the breakdown of the relationship. This fear can lead to clinginess, possessiveness, or a constant anxiety about the future. The fear of loss can also create a sense of desperation in the relationship, where we become overly dependent on the other person for our sense of security and well-being.

5. Fear of Intimacy: The fear of intimacy is the fear of getting too close to someone emotionally, physically, or spiritually. This fear is often rooted in past experiences of hurt, betrayal, or trauma, which have created a reluctance to trust others or to allow them to get close. The fear of intimacy can manifest as a reluctance to commit, an avoidance of deep emotional connection, or a tendency to sabotage relationships when they become too close.

6. Fear of Conflict: The fear of conflict is the fear that disagreements or confrontations in a relationship will lead to harm, rejection, or the end of the relationship. This fear often leads to avoidance of difficult conversations, a tendency to suppress emotions, or a reluctance to express one's needs and desires. The fear of conflict can create a superficial sense of peace in the relationship, but it ultimately undermines true intimacy and trust.

7. Fear of Judgment: The fear of judgment is the fear that others will judge us harshly or negatively for our thoughts, actions, or choices. This fear can lead to a reluctance to be honest, a tendency to conform to others' expectations, or a desire to present a false or idealized version of ourselves. The fear of judgment can prevent us from being authentic and can create a sense of isolation and loneliness in the relationship.

Each of these forms of fear can have a significant impact on relationships, creating barriers to love, intimacy, and connection. However, the good news is that these fears can be overcome through the power of love—specifically, the perfect love that comes from God.

Overcoming Fear with Perfect Love

Overcoming fear in relationships requires a deep understanding of and reliance on the perfect love that casts out fear. This perfect love is rooted in our relationship with God and is cultivated through our growing understanding of His love for us and our ability to extend that love to others. Here are some practical steps to overcome fear with love:

1. Embrace God's Unconditional Love: The foundation for overcoming fear is to fully embrace and internalize God's unconditional love for you. This involves meditating on the truths of Scripture that affirm God's love, such as Romans 8:38-39, which declares that nothing can separate us from the love of God in Christ Jesus. When you are secure in God's love, you are less likely to be controlled by fear, as you know that your identity and worth are rooted in His love, not in the approval or acceptance of others.

2. Cultivate Self-Acceptance: Overcoming the fear of rejection begins with accepting yourself as God accepts you. This means recognizing that you are a beloved child of God, created in His image, and that you are valuable and worthy of love just as you are. Self-acceptance allows you to approach relationships with confidence, knowing that your worth is not dependent on the opinions or actions of others. It also frees you to be authentic and vulnerable in your relationships, without the fear of being rejected.

3. Practice Vulnerability: Vulnerability is the gateway to intimacy in relationships, and overcoming the fear of vulnerability requires practice. Start by gradually opening up to others, sharing your thoughts, feelings, and

experiences in a safe and supportive environment. As you practice vulnerability, you will begin to experience the deep connection and trust that comes from being open and authentic with others. Remember that vulnerability is not a sign of weakness but a strength that allows you to build deeper and more meaningful relationships.

4. Trust in God's Sovereignty: The fear of loss can be overwhelming, especially in relationships that are deeply meaningful to us. However, trusting in God's sovereignty and His plan for your life can help to alleviate this fear. Recognize that God is in control of all things, and that He works all things together for the good of those who love Him (Romans 8:28). Trusting in God's sovereignty allows you to release your fears and to focus on loving and cherishing the people in your life, rather than being consumed by anxiety about the future.

5. Embrace the Growth Process: Overcoming the fear of failure involves embracing the growth process in relationships. Recognize that no one is perfect, and that relationships are opportunities for growth, learning, and mutual support. Instead of fearing failure, approach relationships with a growth mindset, where mistakes and challenges are seen as opportunities to learn and to become better partners, friends, or family members. This mindset allows you to approach relationships with confidence and resilience, knowing that you are continually growing and improving.

6. Prioritize Communication: The fear of conflict can be overcome by prioritizing open and honest communication in relationships. Instead of avoiding difficult conversations, approach them with a spirit of love, respect, and a desire for resolution. Effective communication involves active listening, empathy, and a willingness to understand the other person's perspective. By addressing conflicts openly and lovingly, you can build trust and deepen the connection in the relationship, rather than allowing fear to create distance.

7. Release the Need for Control: The fear of intimacy is often rooted in a desire to control the relationship and to protect oneself from potential hurt. However, true intimacy requires a willingness to release control and to trust in the process of the relationship. This involves being open to the unknown, allowing yourself to be fully present in the relationship, and trusting that God is guiding and protecting you. By releasing the need for control, you create space for love and intimacy to flourish.

8. Seek Healing for Past Wounds: Many fears in relationships are rooted in past experiences of hurt, betrayal, or trauma. Seeking healing for these wounds is essential for overcoming fear and allowing love to thrive. This may involve seeking counseling, engaging in prayer and spiritual practices, or participating in support groups. Healing from past wounds allows you to approach relationships with a fresh perspective, free from the fears and patterns of the past.

9. Practice Forgiveness: The fear of judgment and rejection often stems from a lack of forgiveness—both for yourself and for others. Practicing forgiveness involves releasing the pain, resentment, and judgment that you may be holding onto, and choosing to extend grace to yourself and others. Forgiveness is an act of love that frees you from the burden of fear and allows you to experience the fullness of love in your relationships.

10. Rely on the Holy Spirit: Overcoming fear with love is not something that can be done in your own strength; it requires the work of the Holy Spirit in your life. The Holy Spirit is the source of perfect love, and He empowers you to love others as God loves you. Through prayer, worship, and surrender to the Holy Spirit, you can experience the transformative power of love that casts out fear and brings healing, peace, and joy to your relationships.

The Impact of Overcoming Fear with Love on Relationships

When fear is overcome by love in relationships, the impact is profound and transformative. Relationships that are free from fear are characterized by trust, openness, and a deep sense of connection. Here are some of the ways in which overcoming fear with love can transform your relationships:

1. Building Trust: Trust is the foundation of any healthy relationship, and overcoming fear with love is essential for building and maintaining trust. When fear is no longer a barrier, both parties are free to be honest, vulnerable, and authentic with each other. This openness fosters trust, as both parties feel safe and secure in the relationship, knowing that they are accepted and loved just as they are.

2. Enhancing Intimacy: Intimacy in relationships is deepened when fear is replaced with love. Overcoming the fear of vulnerability, rejection, or judgment allows both parties to share their true selves with each other, leading to a

deeper emotional, spiritual, and physical connection. This intimacy creates a sense of closeness and unity in the relationship, where both parties feel deeply connected and understood.

3. Fostering Open Communication: Relationships that are free from fear are characterized by open and honest communication. When fear is removed, both parties are more likely to express their thoughts, feelings, and needs without fear of rejection or conflict. This open communication leads to a greater understanding of each other's perspectives, needs, and desires, and it helps to prevent misunderstandings and conflicts.

4. Creating a Safe and Supportive Environment: Overcoming fear with love creates a safe and supportive environment in relationships, where both parties feel valued, respected, and cared for. This environment fosters a sense of security and well-being, allowing both parties to be themselves and to grow and thrive in the relationship. A safe and supportive environment also encourages mutual support and encouragement, where both parties feel empowered to pursue their goals and dreams.

5. Encouraging Growth and Healing: Relationships that are free from fear are more conducive to personal and relational growth. When fear is no longer a barrier, both parties are more likely to take risks, to step out of their comfort zones, and to pursue growth and healing. This growth leads to a deeper and more fulfilling relationship, where both parties continue to evolve and grow together.

6. Promoting Forgiveness and Reconciliation: Overcoming fear with love promotes forgiveness and reconciliation in relationships. When fear is removed, both parties are more likely to extend grace, to seek forgiveness, and to work toward reconciliation when conflicts arise. This forgiveness fosters healing and renewal in the relationship, allowing both parties to move forward with love and grace.

7. Strengthening Commitment: Relationships that are free from fear are marked by a strong sense of commitment. When fear is no longer a barrier, both parties are more likely to remain committed to each other, to work through challenges together, and to invest in the long-term health and well-being of the relationship. This commitment is not based on obligation or duty, but on the deep love and connection that is free from fear.

8. Cultivating Joy and Peace: Overcoming fear with love leads to a sense of joy and peace in relationships. When fear is removed, both parties are free to experience the joy of love and the peace that comes from knowing that they are loved and accepted just as they are. This joy and peace create a positive and uplifting environment in the relationship, where both parties feel happy, content, and fulfilled.

Testimonies of Overcoming Fear with Love in Relationships

The power of love to overcome fear in relationships is not just a concept; it is a reality that has brought healing and transformation to countless individuals and relationships. Here are a few testimonies that illustrate the impact of overcoming fear with love:

1. Healing from the Fear of Rejection: Sarah had always struggled with the fear of rejection in her relationships. She had experienced rejection in her childhood, and this fear had carried over into her adult relationships, leading her to avoid vulnerability and to put up walls. However, through counseling and prayer, Sarah began to experience the love of God in a new way. She realized that her worth and identity were rooted in God's love, not in the acceptance of others. As she embraced this truth, her fear of rejection began to diminish, and she was able to approach her relationships with confidence and openness. Today, Sarah enjoys deep and meaningful connections with others, free from the fear of rejection.

2. Overcoming the Fear of Vulnerability in Marriage: John and Lisa had been married for several years, but they struggled with intimacy in their relationship. Both had a fear of vulnerability, which led to emotional distance and a lack of deep connection. After attending a marriage retreat, they learned about the importance of vulnerability in building intimacy and trust. They committed to being more open and honest with each other, sharing their thoughts, feelings, and fears. As they practiced vulnerability, they began to experience a deeper connection and a renewed sense of intimacy in their marriage. Today, John and Lisa's marriage is stronger than ever, and they credit the power of love to overcome their fear of vulnerability.

3. Finding Freedom from the Fear of Failure: David had always been driven by a fear of failure in his relationships. He felt that he had to be perfect in

order to be loved and accepted, which led to perfectionism, stress, and anxiety. However, through a study of God's Word and the encouragement of a mentor, David began to understand that God's love for him was not based on his performance, but on grace. As he embraced this truth, he was able to let go of his fear of failure and to approach his relationships with a sense of freedom and joy. Today, David is more relaxed and confident in his relationships, knowing that he is loved unconditionally by God.

4. Releasing the Fear of Loss: Mary had experienced the loss of a loved one in the past, which left her with a deep fear of losing someone else she loved. This fear led her to become clingy and anxious in her relationships, always worried about the possibility of losing the people she cared about. However, through prayer and reflection, Mary learned to trust in God's sovereignty and to surrender her fears to Him. She realized that God was in control of her life and that His love was greater than her fears. As she released her fear of loss, she was able to experience a deeper sense of peace and contentment in her relationships, knowing that God was watching over her and her loved ones.

5. Breaking Free from the Fear of Conflict: Tom had always been conflict-averse in his relationships, fearing that disagreements would lead to harm or the end of the relationship. This fear led him to avoid difficult conversations and to suppress his emotions, which created tension and distance in his relationships. However, after attending a conflict resolution workshop, Tom learned that conflict could be an opportunity for growth and deeper connection, rather than something to be feared. He began to approach conflicts with love, respect, and a desire for resolution, rather than avoidance. As a result, Tom's relationships became more open and honest, and he experienced a deeper sense of connection with others.

Conclusion

Overcoming fear with love is a transformative process that leads to deeper, more meaningful, and more fulfilling relationships. As we have seen, fear can manifest in many different forms in relationships, creating barriers to love, intimacy, and connection. However, the good news is that these fears can be overcome through the power of perfect love—the love that comes from God.

In reflecting on 1 John 4:18, "There is no fear in love. But perfect love drives out fear," we are reminded that love is the most powerful force in the universe, capable of casting out fear and bringing healing, peace, and joy to our relationships. When we embrace God's love and allow it to fill our hearts, we are freed from the grip of fear, and we are able to engage in relationships with trust, openness, and vulnerability.

As we seek to overcome fear with love in our relationships, may we be inspired by the example of Christ, who demonstrated perfect love through His life, death, and resurrection. May we practice vulnerability, trust, and forgiveness in our relationships, and may we rely on the Holy Spirit to fill us with the perfect love that casts out fear.

In a world that is often marked by fear and insecurity, the power of love to overcome fear stands as a beacon of hope and healing. As we embrace this love in our relationships, we participate in God's redemptive work, bringing light, hope, and love to a world in need of His perfect love.

Chapter 12: Love as a Reflection of Faith

Introduction

In the Christian life, love and faith are deeply interconnected, each one influencing and reinforcing the other. The Apostle Paul, in his letter to the Galatians, captures this connection succinctly when he writes, "For in Christ Jesus neither circumcision nor uncircumcision has any value. The only thing that counts is faith expressing itself through love" (Galatians 5:6). This verse highlights the idea that true faith is not merely a set of beliefs or rituals but is best demonstrated through acts of love. Love, therefore, is not just an emotion or a virtue; it is a tangible expression of the faith that we profess.

In this chapter, we will explore the profound relationship between love and faith, reflecting on how love serves as a reflection of our faith in God and how faith, in turn, empowers us to love others as Christ loves us. We will delve into the theological significance of this connection, examine how love manifests as a practical outworking of faith in various aspects of life, and provide practical guidance on how to cultivate a life where faith and love are inseparable. Through this exploration, we will discover that love is not only the evidence of our faith but also the very means by which our faith is made visible and effective in the world.

The Theological Foundation of Love as a Reflection of Faith

The Bible consistently presents love as the defining characteristic of true faith. Throughout the New Testament, the apostles emphasize that genuine faith in Christ will inevitably produce love—both for God and for others. This connection is not incidental but is rooted in the very nature of God, who is both the source of our faith and the embodiment of perfect love.

In Galatians 5:6, Paul asserts that "the only thing that counts is faith expressing itself through love." This statement comes in the context of a discussion about the nature of true righteousness. Paul is addressing the issue of circumcision, a physical ritual that was highly valued in Jewish religious practice. However, Paul argues that external rituals, whether circumcision or uncircumcision, are ultimately of no value in the Christian life. What matters, he says, is the inward reality of faith that is demonstrated through love.

This idea is echoed in James 2:14-17, where the apostle James writes, "What good is it, my brothers and sisters, if someone claims to have faith but has no deeds? Can such faith save them? Suppose a brother or a sister is without clothes and daily food. If one of you says to them, 'Go in peace; keep warm and well fed,' but does nothing about their physical needs, what good is it? In the same way, faith by itself, if it is not accompanied by action, is dead." James emphasizes that faith without love—without action—is empty and meaningless. True faith is alive and active, and it is most clearly expressed in acts of love and compassion.

Theologically, this connection between faith and love is grounded in the character of God. In 1 John 4:8, we read that "God is love." This means that love is not just one of God's attributes; it is His very essence. Therefore, when we place our faith in God, we are placing our faith in love itself. To believe in God is to believe in love, and to follow God is to live a life characterized by love.

Moreover, the incarnation of Jesus Christ—the ultimate expression of God's love for humanity—demonstrates that true faith leads to sacrificial love. In Philippians 2:5-8, Paul describes how Jesus, though He was in the form of God, did not consider equality with God something to be used to His own advantage. Instead, He humbled Himself, taking on the form of a servant, and became obedient to death on a cross. This act of love is the ultimate example of faith in action, showing that true faith involves a willingness to lay down one's life for the sake of others.

Therefore, love is not just an optional aspect of the Christian life; it is the very evidence of our faith. As Jesus Himself taught, "By this everyone will know that you are my disciples, if you love one another" (John 13:35). Our love for others is the proof of our faith in Christ, and it is through love that our faith is made visible to the world.

Manifesting Love as an Outworking of Faith

The relationship between faith and love is not just a theological concept; it is meant to be lived out in practical ways in every aspect of life. When faith is genuine, it naturally produces love, and this love manifests in various forms and actions that reflect the character of Christ. Here are some of the ways in which love can be manifested as an outworking of faith:

1. Love in Action: Faith that is expressed through love is active and dynamic. It moves beyond mere words or feelings and translates into tangible actions that serve others. This could involve acts of kindness, such as helping those in need, offering support to someone going through a difficult time, or simply being present with someone who is lonely. When we put our faith into action through love, we demonstrate the reality of our faith and bring the love of Christ to those around us.

2. Love in Sacrifice: True love often involves sacrifice—giving of ourselves, our time, our resources, or even our comfort for the sake of others. This sacrificial love is a reflection of the love of Christ, who gave Himself for us. When we willingly make sacrifices for others, we are living out our faith in a way that honors God and serves as a witness to His love. Whether it's sacrificing our time to volunteer, giving financially to support someone in need, or making personal sacrifices to maintain peace in a relationship, sacrificial love is a powerful expression of faith.

3. Love in Forgiveness: Forgiveness is one of the most profound expressions of love and faith. It requires us to let go of our right to seek revenge or to hold onto bitterness and instead to extend grace and mercy to those who have wronged us. Forgiveness is a reflection of the faith we have in God's forgiveness of our own sins and His command to love others as He has loved us. When we forgive, we are demonstrating our trust in God's justice and His ability to bring healing and reconciliation to our relationships.

4. Love in Humility: Humility is a key characteristic of Christlike love, and it is deeply connected to faith. When we love with humility, we are placing the needs and well-being of others above our own, trusting that God will take care of us. Humility allows us to serve others without seeking recognition or praise, to listen and learn from others, and to approach relationships with a spirit of gentleness and respect. This humble love is a reflection of our faith in God's sovereignty and our desire to honor Him by loving others selflessly.

5. Love in Patience: Patience is another important manifestation of love that is rooted in faith. Patience involves trusting God's timing and His plan for our lives and the lives of others. When we are patient with others, we are expressing our faith in God's ability to work in their lives and to bring about His purposes in His own time. Patience in love means being willing to endure difficult situations, to wait for others to grow and change, and to extend grace

even when it's hard. This patient love reflects our faith in God's goodness and His power to bring about transformation.

6. Love in Compassion: Compassion is a deep sense of empathy and concern for the suffering of others, and it is a natural outflow of faith that is rooted in love. When we have faith in God's love and care for us, we are moved to extend that same love and care to others, especially those who are hurting or in need. Compassionate love involves reaching out to those who are suffering, offering comfort and support, and taking action to alleviate their pain. This compassion is a reflection of our faith in God's compassion for us and His call to love our neighbors as ourselves.

7. Love in Truth: Love that is rooted in faith is also committed to truth. This means being honest and transparent in our relationships, speaking the truth in love, and standing up for what is right. Love in truth involves being faithful to God's Word and living according to His standards, even when it's difficult. It also means holding others accountable in a loving and respectful way, helping them to grow in their faith and walk with God. This love in truth is a reflection of our faith in God's truth and our commitment to living out His commands.

8. Love in Service: Service is one of the most tangible expressions of love that flows from faith. When we serve others, we are following the example of Christ, who came not to be served but to serve and to give His life as a ransom for many (Mark 10:45). Service involves using our gifts, talents, and resources to meet the needs of others, to build up the body of Christ, and to glorify God. Whether it's serving in the church, in the community, or in our families, service is a powerful way to demonstrate our faith and to show the love of Christ to the world.

9. Love in Perseverance: Perseverance in love is a reflection of our faith in God's promises and His faithfulness to us. It involves continuing to love and serve others even when it's difficult, when we face obstacles, or when we don't see immediate results. Perseverance in love means being steadfast in our commitments, being faithful in our relationships, and trusting that God is at work even when we can't see it. This perseverance is a reflection of our faith in God's ability to bring about His purposes and to sustain us through all circumstances.

10. Love in Joy: Finally, love that is rooted in faith is characterized by joy. This joy comes from knowing that we are loved by God and that we have the privilege of sharing that love with others. Joyful love involves delighting in others, celebrating their successes, and finding joy in serving and blessing them. This joy is a reflection of our faith in God's goodness and His desire for us to experience the fullness of life in Him. Joyful love is contagious, and it brings light and life to our relationships and communities.

The Inseparable Connection Between Faith and Love

The connection between faith and love is not only theological but also deeply practical. In the Christian life, faith and love are inseparable; one cannot exist without the other. Genuine faith will always produce love, and true love is always rooted in faith. Here are some key ways in which faith and love are interconnected:

1. Faith Empowers Love: Faith in God empowers us to love others as Christ loves us. When we place our trust in God's love, we are freed from the need to seek validation, approval, or security from others. This freedom allows us to love others selflessly, without fear of rejection or loss. Faith also gives us the strength to love even when it's difficult, to forgive when we've been wronged, and to serve others with joy and gratitude. In this way, faith is the foundation and the fuel for love.

2. Love Validates Faith: Love serves as the evidence of our faith. As James writes, "Faith by itself, if it is not accompanied by action, is dead" (James 2:17). True faith will always manifest in love—both for God and for others. When we love others, we are demonstrating the reality of our faith and showing the world that we belong to Christ. Love is the fruit of faith, and it is through love that our faith is made visible and effective.

3. Faith Sustains Love: In the face of challenges, difficulties, and trials, it is faith that sustains our love. When we encounter obstacles in our relationships or in our efforts to love others, it is our faith in God's promises and His faithfulness that gives us the strength to persevere. Faith reminds us that God is with us, that He is working all things together for our good, and that His love never fails. This faith sustains our love and enables us to keep loving, even when it's hard.

4. Love Strengthens Faith: Love, in turn, strengthens our faith. When we experience the love of God and the love of others, our faith is deepened and strengthened. Love builds trust, creates a sense of security, and fosters a deeper connection with God and with others. As we love and are loved, our faith grows, and we become more rooted and grounded in God's love. This deepened faith then enables us to love even more fully and freely.

5. Faith and Love Reflect God's Character: Both faith and love reflect the character of God. God is both faithful and loving, and He calls us to reflect His character in our lives. When we live by faith and express that faith through love, we are imitating God and showing the world what He is like. Our faith and love serve as a testimony to God's goodness, His faithfulness, and His love for all people.

6. Faith and Love Fulfill the Law: In Galatians 5:14, Paul writes, "For the entire law is fulfilled in keeping this one command: 'Love your neighbor as yourself.'" This statement underscores the idea that love is the fulfillment of the law and that faith, when expressed through love, fulfills God's commandments. When we live by faith and love others as Christ loves us, we are fulfilling God's law and living in accordance with His will.

7. Faith and Love Lead to Spiritual Growth: Finally, the connection between faith and love is essential for spiritual growth. As we grow in our faith, we are empowered to love more deeply, more selflessly, and more sacrificially. This love, in turn, leads to greater spiritual maturity, as we become more like Christ in our character and conduct. The relationship between faith and love is a dynamic one, where each one feeds and strengthens the other, leading to continual growth and transformation in the Christian life.

Cultivating a Life Where Faith and Love Are Inseparable

Cultivating a life where faith and love are inseparable requires intentionality, commitment, and a reliance on God's grace. Here are some practical steps to help you live out the connection between faith and love in your daily life:

1. Deepen Your Relationship with God: The foundation for a life of faith and love is a deep and personal relationship with God. Spend time in prayer, worship, and the study of God's Word to grow in your knowledge of His love

and faithfulness. As you deepen your relationship with God, your faith will be strengthened, and you will be empowered to love others more fully.

2. Practice Love in Action: Make it a priority to put your faith into action through acts of love. Look for opportunities to serve others, to show kindness, and to meet the needs of those around you. Whether it's helping a neighbor, volunteering in your community, or offering a listening ear to a friend, let your love be the evidence of your faith.

3. Cultivate a Heart of Humility: Humility is essential for both faith and love. Cultivate a heart of humility by placing the needs of others above your own, by being willing to learn from others, and by serving others without seeking recognition. Humility allows you to love selflessly and to trust in God's plan for your life.

4. Practice Forgiveness and Grace: Forgiveness is a powerful expression of love that is rooted in faith. Practice forgiveness by letting go of past hurts, extending grace to those who have wronged you, and seeking reconciliation in your relationships. Forgiveness reflects your faith in God's forgiveness of your own sins and your commitment to loving others as Christ loves you.

5. Seek to Grow in Love: Make it a priority to grow in your capacity to love others. This might involve studying the Scriptures to understand what true love looks like, seeking out mentors or role models who exemplify Christlike love, or participating in small groups or classes that focus on spiritual growth and discipleship. As you seek to grow in love, your faith will be strengthened, and your relationships will be enriched.

6. Trust in God's Sovereignty: Trusting in God's sovereignty is essential for overcoming the fears and challenges that can hinder love. When you encounter obstacles in your relationships or in your efforts to love others, trust that God is in control and that He is working all things together for your good. This trust will sustain your love and enable you to persevere, even in difficult circumstances.

7. Reflect on God's Love for You: Take time to reflect on the love that God has shown you through Christ. Meditate on the sacrifice that Jesus made on the cross, the forgiveness that you have received, and the grace that has been extended to you. As you reflect on God's love for you, let it inspire and motivate you to love others with the same kind of sacrificial and unconditional love.

8. Live with Joy and Gratitude: Joy and gratitude are key components of a life where faith and love are inseparable. Cultivate a spirit of joy and gratitude by focusing on the blessings that God has given you, by celebrating the love and relationships in your life, and by expressing your thanks to God and to others. Joyful love is a powerful testimony to the goodness of God and the reality of your faith.

9. Engage in Community: Surround yourself with a community of believers who encourage and support you in your walk of faith and love. Engage in fellowship, worship, and service with others who share your commitment to Christ. Being part of a community allows you to grow in your faith, to practice love in tangible ways, and to receive the support and encouragement that you need to live out your faith.

10. Surrender to the Holy Spirit: Finally, surrender to the work of the Holy Spirit in your life. The Holy Spirit is the source of both faith and love, and He empowers you to live a life where these two are inseparable. Pray for the Holy Spirit to fill you with His love, to strengthen your faith, and to guide you in your relationships with others. Trust that the Holy Spirit will lead you in the path of love and faith, and that He will produce the fruit of love in your life.

The Impact of Living a Life Where Faith and Love Are Inseparable

When faith and love are inseparable in our lives, the impact is profound and far-reaching. A life characterized by faith and love not only transforms our own hearts and minds but also has a powerful influence on those around us. Here are some of the ways in which living a life where faith and love are inseparable can impact your life and the lives of others:

1. Personal Transformation: When faith and love are inseparable in your life, you experience personal transformation as you become more like Christ in your character and conduct. Your heart is softened, your attitudes and behaviors are shaped by love, and your faith is strengthened. This transformation leads to greater spiritual maturity, a deeper relationship with God, and a more fulfilling and purposeful life.

2. Stronger Relationships: A life where faith and love are inseparable leads to stronger and healthier relationships. When your faith is expressed through

love, you build trust, create a sense of security, and foster deep connections with others. Your relationships become a source of joy, support, and encouragement, and you are able to navigate challenges with grace and resilience.

3. Positive Influence on Others: When faith and love are inseparable in your life, you become a positive influence on those around you. Your love and faith serve as a testimony to the goodness of God and the reality of the Gospel. Others are drawn to the light and love that you reflect, and you have the opportunity to impact their lives in meaningful and lasting ways.

4. Fulfillment of God's Purpose: A life characterized by faith and love fulfills God's purpose for your life. You are able to live in alignment with His will, to glorify Him in all that you do, and to participate in His redemptive work in the world. Your life becomes a living testimony to the power of God's love and the reality of His kingdom.

Legacy of Love: Finally, living a life where faith and love are inseparable leaves a lasting legacy of love. The love that you express through your faith has a ripple effect, impacting not only your immediate relationships but also future generations. Your legacy of love becomes a testimony to the power of God's love and a source of inspiration for others to follow in your footsteps.

Conclusion

Love and faith are inseparable in the Christian life, each one influencing and reinforcing the other. As we have seen, love is not just an emotion or a virtue; it is a tangible expression of our faith in God and a reflection of His character. Faith, in turn, empowers us to love others as Christ loves us, enabling us to live lives that are marked by humility, sacrifice, service, and joy.

In reflecting on Galatians 5:6, "The only thing that counts is faith expressing itself through love," we are reminded that true faith is always accompanied by love and that this love is the evidence of our faith. When we live by faith and express that faith through love, we are fulfilling God's commandments, reflecting His character, and participating in His redemptive work in the world.

As we seek to cultivate a life where faith and love are inseparable, may we be inspired by the example of Christ, who demonstrated the ultimate expression of faith and love through His life, death, and resurrection. May we put our faith into action through acts of love, and may we trust in God's grace to empower us to live lives that are marked by faith, love, and joy.

In a world that is often marked by division, fear, and self-interest, the power of faith expressing itself through love stands as a beacon of hope and healing. As we embrace this connection in our lives, we participate in God's redemptive work, bringing light, love, and faith to a world in need of His grace.

Chapter 13: The Eternal Nature of Love

Introduction

Love is a word that carries profound meaning and significance in the Christian faith. It is not just an emotion or a temporary feeling; it is the very essence of God and the foundation of all relationships that are rooted in Him. In 1 Corinthians 13:8, the Apostle Paul declares, "Love never fails." This simple yet powerful statement encapsulates the eternal nature of divine love—a love that is unchanging, enduring, and everlasting. Unlike human accomplishments, knowledge, or spiritual gifts, which may fade or cease, love remains forever. It is this eternal quality of love that sets it apart as the greatest of all virtues and the most enduring aspect of our relationships with God and others.

In this chapter, we will explore the concept of the eternal nature of love, reflecting on how divine love transcends time and continues to exist beyond the temporal realm. We will delve into the theological significance of this eternal love, examine how it can shape and guide our relationships, and provide practical guidance on how to build relationships that reflect the eternal quality of God's love. Through this exploration, we will discover that love, as defined and demonstrated by God, is not only the foundation of our faith but also the key to building relationships that last beyond this life and into eternity.

The Theological Foundation of the Eternal Nature of Love

The eternal nature of love is rooted in the very character of God. Throughout the Bible, God is described as love itself, and His love is portrayed as everlasting, unchanging, and infinite. In 1 John 4:16, we read, "God is love. Whoever lives in love lives in God, and God in them." This verse underscores the idea that love is not just one of God's attributes but is the very essence of His being. Because God is eternal, His love is also eternal, and it transcends time, space, and all human limitations.

In 1 Corinthians 13, often referred to as the "Love Chapter," Paul provides a detailed description of the qualities of love and emphasizes its enduring nature. After describing the characteristics of love—patience, kindness, humility, selflessness, forgiveness, and rejoicing in the truth—Paul concludes by highlighting the eternal nature of love: "Love never fails. But where there are prophecies, they will cease; where there are tongues, they will be stilled; where there is knowledge, it will pass away" (1 Corinthians 13:8). Here, Paul contrasts love with spiritual gifts and human knowledge, which are temporal and will eventually come to an end. In contrast, love is eternal and will continue to exist even when all else fades away.

Theologically, the eternal nature of love is also tied to the concept of God's covenantal love for His people. Throughout the Old Testament, God enters into covenants with His people, promising to be their God and to love them with an everlasting love. In Jeremiah 31:3, God declares, "I have loved you with an everlasting love; I have drawn you with unfailing kindness." This covenantal love is not based on human merit or performance but on God's unchanging nature and His commitment to His people. It is a love that endures through all circumstances, remaining constant even in the face of human unfaithfulness or failure.

In the New Testament, the eternal nature of love is most clearly demonstrated in the life, death, and resurrection of Jesus Christ. Jesus' sacrificial love on the cross is the ultimate expression of God's eternal love for humanity. In John 15:13, Jesus says, "Greater love has no one than this: to lay down one's life for one's friends." This love is not limited to a particular time or place; it is a love that transcends history and continues to impact lives today. The resurrection of Christ further affirms the eternal nature of this love, as it demonstrates that love conquers even death and continues into eternity.

The eternal nature of love is also reflected in the Christian hope of eternal life. In Romans 8:38-39, Paul writes, "For I am convinced that neither death nor life, neither angels nor demons, neither the present nor the future, nor any powers, neither height nor depth, nor anything else in all creation, will be able to separate us from the love of God that is in Christ Jesus our Lord." This passage emphasizes that God's love is not only eternal but also inseparable from those who are in Christ. It is a love that will continue to be experienced in the life to come, as believers enter into eternal communion with God and with one another.

Love as the Foundation for Eternal Relationships

The eternal nature of divine love has profound implications for how we build and nurture our relationships. If love is eternal, then the relationships we form based on that love also have the potential to endure beyond this life. As Christians, we are called to build relationships that reflect the eternal quality of God's love—relationships that are not merely based on fleeting emotions or temporary circumstances but are grounded in the enduring love of Christ.

1. Love as the Basis for Lasting Commitment: One of the most important aspects of eternal love is its ability to sustain lasting commitment in relationships. In a world where relationships are often seen as disposable or temporary, the concept of eternal love challenges us to approach our relationships with a sense of permanence and commitment. Whether in marriage, friendship, or family relationships, eternal love calls us to remain faithful, even when circumstances change or challenges arise. This commitment is not based on feelings or convenience but on the unchanging nature of God's love, which empowers us to love others with the same steadfastness and dedication.

2. Love as the Source of Forgiveness and Reconciliation: Eternal love also provides the foundation for forgiveness and reconciliation in relationships. Because God's love is eternal and unconditional, we are called to extend that same love to others, forgiving them as God has forgiven us. In Matthew 18:21-22, Peter asks Jesus how many times he should forgive someone who sins against him, suggesting "up to seven times." Jesus responds, "I tell you, not seven times, but seventy-seven times." This response emphasizes the limitless nature of forgiveness that is rooted in eternal love. When we forgive, we are participating in the eternal love of God, allowing our relationships to be healed and restored, rather than being broken by unforgiveness or bitterness.

3. Love as the Foundation for Trust and Security: Trust is a vital component of any relationship, and it is built on the foundation of love. When we experience the eternal love of God, we gain a sense of security and trust that enables us to build strong and lasting relationships with others. This trust is not based on human perfection but on the knowledge that God's love is constant and unchanging. As we learn to trust in God's love, we are able to extend that trust to others, creating relationships that are marked by mutual

respect, honesty, and reliability. This trust and security allow relationships to thrive, even in the face of challenges or uncertainties.

4. Love as a Reflection of God's Eternal Kingdom: The relationships we build on the foundation of eternal love are a reflection of God's eternal kingdom. In the Lord's Prayer, Jesus teaches us to pray, "Your kingdom come, your will be done, on earth as it is in heaven" (Matthew 6:10). This prayer reflects the desire for God's eternal kingdom to be manifested in our lives and relationships here on earth. When we build relationships that are based on the eternal love of God, we are participating in the advancement of His kingdom, bringing a taste of heaven to earth. These relationships serve as a testimony to the world of the reality of God's love and His eternal purposes.

5. Love as the Source of Joy and Fulfillment: Eternal love is also the source of deep and lasting joy and fulfillment in relationships. Unlike the fleeting pleasures of this world, the joy that comes from eternal love is enduring and unshakeable. This joy is rooted in the knowledge that we are loved by God with an everlasting love and that our relationships are part of His eternal plan. When we build relationships based on this love, we experience a sense of fulfillment that transcends the ups and downs of life. This joy is not dependent on external circumstances but is grounded in the eternal nature of God's love, which remains constant in all situations.

6. Love as the Motivation for Sacrificial Service: The eternal nature of love also motivates us to serve others selflessly and sacrificially. In John 15:12-13, Jesus commands His disciples, "My command is this: Love each other as I have loved you. Greater love has no one than this: to lay down one's life for one's friends." This call to sacrificial love is rooted in the eternal love of God, which was demonstrated through the sacrifice of Christ on the cross. When we serve others with this kind of love, we are participating in the eternal purposes of God and reflecting His character to the world. This sacrificial service is not a burden but a joy, as it allows us to experience the depth and richness of God's love in our own lives.

Building Relationships That Reflect the Eternal Nature of Love

Building relationships that reflect the eternal nature of love requires intentionality, commitment, and a deep understanding of God's love. Here are some practical steps to help you build relationships that are grounded in the eternal love of God:

1. Anchor Your Relationships in God's Love: The foundation of any relationship that reflects the eternal nature of love must be anchored in God's love. This means making a conscious decision to prioritize your relationship with God and to allow His love to shape and guide your interactions with others. Spend time in prayer, worship, and the study of God's Word to deepen your understanding of His love and to allow it to influence your relationships. As you anchor your relationships in God's love, you will find that they become more resilient, enduring, and life-giving.

2. Practice Unconditional Love: Unconditional love is a hallmark of eternal love. It is a love that is not based on what the other person can do for you or how they make you feel but is rooted in a commitment to love them regardless of circumstances. Practice unconditional love in your relationships by extending grace, forgiveness, and kindness, even when it's difficult. This kind of love reflects the eternal love of God, which is constant and unchanging, and it creates a strong foundation for lasting relationships.

3. Cultivate a Heart of Forgiveness: Forgiveness is essential for building relationships that reflect the eternal nature of love. In a fallen world, misunderstandings, conflicts, and hurts are inevitable, but forgiveness allows relationships to heal and grow stronger. Cultivate a heart of forgiveness by regularly reflecting on the forgiveness that God has extended to you through Christ. Choose to let go of grudges, bitterness, and resentment, and instead, extend grace and mercy to others. This act of forgiveness is a powerful way to participate in the eternal love of God and to build relationships that endure.

4. Commit to Faithfulness and Loyalty: Faithfulness and loyalty are key components of eternal love. In a culture that often promotes self-interest and individualism, committing to faithfulness and loyalty in your relationships can be countercultural. However, these qualities are essential for building relationships that last. Be faithful in your commitments, whether in marriage,

friendship, or family relationships. Show loyalty by standing by those you love, even in difficult times. This faithfulness and loyalty reflect the eternal love of God, which is steadfast and unchanging.

5. Build Relationships on the Foundation of Truth: Truth is a vital component of relationships that reflect the eternal nature of love. Build your relationships on the foundation of truth by being honest, transparent, and trustworthy. Avoid deceit, manipulation, or dishonesty, as these behaviors undermine the integrity of the relationship. Instead, speak the truth in love, even when it's difficult, and be willing to hold yourself and others accountable to the truth. This commitment to truth creates a strong foundation for relationships that endure and reflect the eternal love of God.

6. Serve Others with a Heart of Sacrifice: Sacrificial service is a powerful expression of eternal love. Look for opportunities to serve others selflessly, whether in small acts of kindness or in more significant ways. Be willing to put the needs of others above your own, and serve with a heart of joy and gratitude. This sacrificial service reflects the love of Christ, who gave Himself for us, and it builds relationships that are marked by mutual care and respect. As you serve others, you will find that your relationships become more meaningful and enduring.

7. Prioritize Eternal Values in Your Relationships: Building relationships that reflect the eternal nature of love requires a focus on eternal values, such as love, faith, hope, and righteousness. Prioritize these values in your relationships by focusing on what truly matters in light of eternity. Avoid getting caught up in temporary concerns or distractions, and instead, invest in the spiritual growth and well-being of those you love. This focus on eternal values helps to build relationships that are aligned with God's purposes and that will last beyond this life.

8. Pray for God's Guidance and Blessing: Prayer is essential for building relationships that reflect the eternal nature of love. Regularly pray for God's guidance and blessing in your relationships, asking Him to help you love others as He loves you. Pray for wisdom, patience, and understanding, and seek God's will in all your interactions. As you commit your relationships to God in prayer, you will find that His love and grace are poured out in abundance, strengthening and sustaining your relationships.

9. Foster a Spirit of Gratitude and Joy: Gratitude and joy are natural outflows of eternal love. Foster a spirit of gratitude and joy in your relationships by regularly expressing thanks to God and to those you love. Celebrate the blessings and joys of your relationships, and find joy in the presence of those you care about. This spirit of gratitude and joy reflects the eternal nature of God's love, which is a source of deep and lasting happiness.

10. Live with an Eternal Perspective: Finally, live with an eternal perspective in your relationships. Recognize that the love you share with others is part of God's eternal plan and that your relationships have the potential to impact eternity. Approach your relationships with a sense of purpose and intentionality, seeking to glorify God and to advance His kingdom through the love you share. This eternal perspective helps to keep your relationships focused on what truly matters and encourages you to invest in relationships that will endure beyond this life.

The Impact of Building Relationships That Reflect the Eternal Nature of Love

When we build relationships that reflect the eternal nature of love, the impact is profound and far-reaching. These relationships not only bring joy, fulfillment, and purpose to our lives but also serve as a powerful testimony to the world of the reality of God's love. Here are some of the ways in which building relationships that reflect the eternal nature of love can impact your life and the lives of others:

1. Deepening of Spiritual Growth: Relationships that are built on the foundation of eternal love contribute to your spiritual growth and maturity. As you learn to love others with the same love that God has for you, you become more like Christ in your character and conduct. This deepening of spiritual growth leads to a closer relationship with God and a greater understanding of His will for your life.

2. Strengthening of Family Bonds: The eternal nature of love has a powerful impact on family relationships. When families prioritize eternal love, they create an environment of trust, security, and mutual support. This strengthens the bonds between family members and helps to create a legacy of love that is passed down through generations. Families that are rooted in eternal love are

better equipped to navigate challenges and to support one another in times of need.

3. Enrichment of Friendships: Friendships that are built on the foundation of eternal love are characterized by loyalty, trust, and deep connection. These friendships provide a source of joy, encouragement, and support throughout life's journey. When friendships are grounded in eternal love, they are more likely to endure through the ups and downs of life, providing a stable and lasting source of companionship.

4. Promotion of Peace and Reconciliation: Relationships that reflect the eternal nature of love are more likely to promote peace and reconciliation. When love is eternal, it is patient, forgiving, and willing to go the extra mile to restore broken relationships. This commitment to reconciliation helps to build a culture of peace and understanding, both in personal relationships and in the broader community.

5. Witness to the World: Relationships that are marked by eternal love serve as a powerful witness to the world of the reality of God's love. In a world that is often characterized by division, conflict, and selfishness, relationships that reflect God's eternal love stand out as a testimony to the transforming power of the Gospel. These relationships draw others to Christ, as they see the love of God lived out in practical and tangible ways.

6. Preparation for Eternity: Finally, building relationships that reflect the eternal nature of love prepares you for eternity. The love you cultivate in this life is a foretaste of the love you will experience in the presence of God for all eternity. By investing in relationships that are grounded in eternal love, you are storing up treasures in heaven and participating in God's eternal kingdom.

Testimonies of Relationships Reflecting the Eternal Nature of Love

Throughout history, there have been countless examples of relationships that reflect the eternal nature of love. These relationships serve as powerful testimonies to the enduring and transformative power of God's love. Here are a few testimonies that illustrate the impact of building relationships that reflect the eternal nature of love:

1. A Marriage Grounded in Eternal Love: Tom and Susan had been married for over 50 years, and their relationship was a testament to the eternal nature of love. Throughout their marriage, they faced many challenges, including health issues, financial difficulties, and the loss of loved ones. However, their love for each other remained constant, grounded in their shared faith in God and their commitment to love each other unconditionally. Their marriage was marked by forgiveness, sacrifice, and mutual support, and it served as an inspiration to everyone who knew them. Even in their later years, their love continued to grow, and they looked forward to spending eternity together in the presence of God.

2. A Friendship That Withstood the Test of Time: Emily and Sarah had been friends since childhood, and their friendship was built on a foundation of eternal love. Over the years, they supported each other through the highs and lows of life, always standing by each other's side. Their friendship was characterized by honesty, loyalty, and a deep sense of connection. Even when they lived in different parts of the country, their friendship remained strong, as they regularly prayed for each other and encouraged each other in their walk with God. Their friendship was a source of joy and strength for both of them, and they knew that their bond would continue into eternity.

3. A Family United by Eternal Love: The Johnson family was known in their community for their strong family bonds and their commitment to living out their faith. The parents, Mark and Lisa, had raised their children with a deep understanding of God's love and the importance of loving others. As their children grew up and started families of their own, the Johnson family remained close-knit, regularly gathering for family meals, prayer, and fellowship. Their family relationships were marked by forgiveness, generosity, and a willingness to support each other in times of need. The Johnson family's love for each other was a reflection of God's eternal love, and it served as a powerful witness to their neighbors and friends.

4. Reconciliation Through Eternal Love: John and his brother, Michael, had been estranged for many years due to a family conflict. The hurt and bitterness between them seemed insurmountable, and neither was willing to take the first step toward reconciliation. However, after experiencing a powerful encounter with God's love, John felt convicted to reach out to his brother and seek reconciliation. With God's help, they were able to forgive each

other and rebuild their relationship. Their reconciliation was a testament to the eternal nature of God's love, which has the power to heal even the deepest wounds. Today, John and Michael's relationship is stronger than ever, and they are committed to loving and supporting each other for the rest of their lives.

5. A Legacy of Love Passed Down Through Generations: The Davis family had a long history of strong family relationships, and their love for each other had been passed down through generations. The family patriarch, Henry Davis, had instilled in his children and grandchildren the importance of loving God and loving others. Even after his passing, his legacy of love continued to impact his family. The Davis family remained close-knit, regularly gathering for family reunions and supporting each other in times of need. The love that Henry had modeled for his family was a reflection of God's eternal love, and it continued to bear fruit in the lives of his descendants.

Conclusion

The eternal nature of love is one of the most profound and transformative aspects of the Christian faith. As we have seen, love is not just an emotion or a temporary feeling; it is the very essence of God and the foundation of all relationships that are rooted in Him. The eternal nature of divine love challenges us to build relationships that reflect this eternal quality—relationships that are not merely based on fleeting emotions or temporary circumstances but are grounded in the enduring love of Christ.

In reflecting on 1 Corinthians 13:8, "Love never fails," we are reminded that love is the most enduring aspect of our lives and relationships. It is a love that transcends time, space, and all human limitations—a love that will continue to exist even when all else fades away. As we seek to build relationships that reflect this eternal love, may we be inspired by the example of Christ, who demonstrated the ultimate expression of eternal love through His life, death, and resurrection.

As we cultivate relationships that are grounded in the eternal love of God, we participate in His redemptive work, bringing light, hope, and love to a world in need of His grace. These relationships not only bring joy, fulfillment, and purpose to our lives but also serve as a powerful testimony to the world of the reality of God's love. And as we live out this eternal love in our relationships, we prepare ourselves for eternity, where we will experience the fullness of God's love for all time.

Chapter 14: Love as a Witness

Introduction

In the Christian faith, love is not only a commandment but also a defining characteristic that distinguishes believers from the rest of the world. Jesus emphasized the importance of love in the lives of His followers, stating, "A new command I give you: Love one another. As I have loved you, so you must love one another. By this, everyone will know that you are my disciples, if you love one another" (John 13:34-35). These words highlight the role of love as a powerful witness to the reality of Christ in the life of a believer. It is through love that the world sees the transformative power of the Gospel and is drawn to the light of Christ.

In this chapter, we will explore the concept of love as a witness, reflecting on how the love of Christ, expressed through believers, serves as a testimony to the world. We will delve into the theological significance of love as a witness, examine the practical ways in which love can be demonstrated in our daily lives, and provide guidance on how to cultivate a love that reflects the reality of Christ. Through this exploration, we will discover that love is not only a personal virtue but also a powerful tool for evangelism and a means of glorifying God in the world.

The Theological Foundation of Love as a Witness

The idea of love as a witness is deeply rooted in the teachings of Jesus and the New Testament. Throughout His ministry, Jesus consistently taught that love is the greatest commandment and the hallmark of true discipleship. In Matthew 22:37-40, Jesus summarizes the entire Law and the Prophets with two commandments: "'Love the Lord your God with all your heart and with all your soul and with all your mind.' This is the first and greatest commandment. And the second is like it: 'Love your neighbor as yourself.'" These commandments emphasize that love is the essence of the Christian life and the foundation upon which all other aspects of faith are built.

In John 13:34-35, Jesus introduces a "new commandment" to His disciples, calling them to love one another as He has loved them. This commandment is not new in the sense that it replaces the Old Testament commandments to love God and neighbor, but it is new in its depth and scope. Jesus is calling His disciples to love with the same sacrificial, selfless, and unconditional love that He has demonstrated through His life and ministry. This love is to be the distinguishing mark of His followers, setting them apart from the world and serving as a powerful witness to the reality of Christ.

Theologically, love as a witness is closely tied to the concept of the incarnation. In the incarnation, God became flesh and dwelt among us in the person of Jesus Christ. Through His life, death, and resurrection, Jesus revealed the fullness of God's love for humanity. In John 1:14, we read, "The Word became flesh and made his dwelling among us. We have seen his glory, the glory of the one and only Son, who came from the Father, full of grace and truth." The incarnation is the ultimate expression of God's love, and it is through this love that the world comes to know and experience the reality of God.

As followers of Christ, believers are called to continue this incarnational ministry by embodying the love of Christ in their lives. When believers love one another and love their neighbors, they are participating in the ongoing revelation of God's love to the world. This love serves as a witness to the reality of Christ, demonstrating that He is alive and at work in the lives of His followers. In this way, love is not just a personal virtue but a powerful testimony that points others to the truth of the Gospel.

The Witness of Love in the Early Church

The early Christian church understood the importance of love as a witness, and this understanding shaped their communities and their outreach to the world. The book of Acts provides numerous examples of how the early believers lived out their faith through acts of love and service, and how this love served as a powerful witness to those around them.

In Acts 2:42-47, we read about the early Christian community: "They devoted themselves to the apostles' teaching and to fellowship, to the breaking of bread and to prayer. Everyone was filled with awe at the many wonders and signs performed by the apostles. All the believers were together and had everything in common. They sold property and possessions to give to anyone who had need. Every day they continued to meet together in the temple courts. They broke bread in their homes and ate together with glad and sincere hearts, praising God and enjoying the favor of all the people. And the Lord added to their number daily those who were being saved." This passage highlights the love and unity that characterized the early church, as well as the impact this love had on those outside the community. The believers' love for one another and their willingness to share their resources with those in need served as a powerful witness, drawing others to the faith.

Similarly, in Acts 4:32-35, we see another example of the early church's commitment to love and generosity: "All the believers were one in heart and mind. No one claimed that any of their possessions was their own, but they shared everything they had. With great power the apostles continued to testify to the resurrection of the Lord Jesus. And God's grace was so powerfully at work in them all that there were no needy persons among them. For from time to time those who owned land or houses sold them, brought the money from the sales and put it at the apostles' feet, and it was distributed to anyone who had need." This passage illustrates how the early Christians' love for one another was a reflection of God's grace at work in their lives. Their love and generosity not only met the physical needs of the community but also served as a testimony to the transformative power of the Gospel.

The witness of love in the early church was not limited to acts of charity and generosity; it also extended to their relationships with one another and with those outside the faith. In a world marked by division, conflict, and social stratification, the early Christians' commitment to love and unity set them apart. Their love for one another transcended social, ethnic, and economic boundaries, creating a community that reflected the inclusive and reconciling love of Christ. This love served as a powerful witness to the world, demonstrating that in Christ, all people are valued and loved, regardless of their background or status.

The early church's witness of love was not without challenges. The believers faced persecution, opposition, and internal conflicts. However, their commitment to love and unity remained steadfast, and it was this love that sustained them through difficult times and enabled them to continue their mission of spreading the Gospel. The early church's example serves as a reminder that love is not just a sentiment but a powerful force that can overcome obstacles, heal divisions, and transform lives.

Practical Ways to Demonstrate Love as a Witness

While the concept of love as a witness is deeply theological, it is also highly practical. Love must be lived out in tangible ways if it is to serve as a witness to the world. Here are some practical ways in which believers can demonstrate love as a witness in their daily lives:

1. Love in Action: One of the most effective ways to demonstrate love as a witness is through acts of service and kindness. Look for opportunities to serve others in your community, whether it's helping a neighbor with chores, volunteering at a local charity, or providing support to someone in need. These acts of love not only meet practical needs but also serve as a testimony to the love of Christ. When others see your willingness to serve selflessly, they are more likely to be drawn to the message of the Gospel.

2. Love in Relationships: The way you relate to others—your family, friends, coworkers, and even strangers—can serve as a powerful witness to the reality of Christ in your life. Cultivate relationships that are marked by love, respect, and humility. Be quick to forgive, slow to anger, and always seek to build others up. In your interactions, strive to reflect the love and grace that you have received from God. When others see the love of Christ reflected in your relationships, they will be more inclined to consider the truth of the Gospel.

3. Love in Words: Your words have the power to build up or tear down, to encourage or discourage, to heal or harm. Use your words to speak life, hope, and encouragement to those around you. Be mindful of how you speak to others, especially in difficult or contentious situations. Let your words be seasoned with grace, and strive to communicate love and truth in all your interactions. When others hear your words of love and kindness, they will be more open to hearing the message of the Gospel.

4. Love in Community: As members of the body of Christ, believers are called to love and support one another within the context of the church community. Participate actively in the life of your church, building relationships with fellow believers and working together to serve the community. The love and unity within the church can serve as a powerful witness to those outside the faith. When the church is a place where people are genuinely loved, accepted, and cared for, it becomes a beacon of hope and light in a world that is often marked by division and isolation.

5. Love in Forgiveness and Reconciliation: One of the most powerful ways to demonstrate love as a witness is through forgiveness and reconciliation. In a world that often seeks revenge or holds onto grudges, the willingness to forgive and seek reconciliation is a radical expression of Christ's love. If there are broken relationships in your life, take the initiative to seek forgiveness and healing. By doing so, you not only restore relationships but also bear witness to the transformative power of God's love. When others see your commitment to forgiveness and reconciliation, they are more likely to be drawn to the message of the Gospel.

6. Love in Generosity: Generosity is a tangible expression of love that can serve as a powerful witness to the world. Look for opportunities to give generously of your time, resources, and talents to those in need. Whether it's supporting a charity, helping a friend in need, or contributing to a church or ministry, your generosity reflects the love of Christ. When others see your willingness to give selflessly, they are more likely to be drawn to the message of the Gospel.

7. Love in Hospitality: Hospitality is another practical way to demonstrate love as a witness. Open your home and your heart to others, offering a warm and welcoming environment where people can experience the love of Christ. Whether it's inviting a neighbor over for a meal, hosting a Bible study, or simply being available to listen and support others, your hospitality can serve as a powerful testimony to the love of Christ. When others experience your genuine hospitality, they are more likely to be open to hearing the message of the Gospel.

8. Love in Integrity: Integrity is an essential aspect of love as a witness. Live your life with honesty, transparency, and moral integrity, reflecting the character of Christ in all that you do. Be consistent in your actions, both in public and in private, and strive to live in a way that honors God. When others see your commitment to integrity, they are more likely to trust and respect you, and they may be more open to hearing the message of the Gospel.

9. Love in Prayer: Prayer is a powerful expression of love that can serve as a witness to the world. Pray regularly for those in your life, including family, friends, coworkers, and neighbors. Pray for their needs, their struggles, and their spiritual growth. When others know that you are praying for them, it can have a profound impact on their lives and open their hearts to the message of

the Gospel. Additionally, praying for others helps to cultivate a heart of love and compassion, making you more attuned to their needs and more willing to serve them.

10. Love in Advocacy: Advocacy is another way to demonstrate love as a witness. Speak out on behalf of those who are marginalized, oppressed, or in need, and work to bring about justice and positive change in your community. Whether it's advocating for the poor, supporting efforts to end human trafficking, or standing up for the rights of the vulnerable, your advocacy reflects the love of Christ and serves as a powerful testimony to the world. When others see your commitment to justice and compassion, they are more likely to be drawn to the message of the Gospel.

The Impact of Love as a Witness

When love is demonstrated as a witness, it has a profound impact on both the individual believer and the broader community. Love as a witness not only strengthens the faith of the believer but also serves as a powerful tool for evangelism and discipleship. Here are some of the ways in which love as a witness can impact your life and the lives of others:

1. Strengthening of Faith: When believers actively demonstrate love as a witness, their faith is strengthened and deepened. Loving others in practical ways requires a reliance on God's grace and strength, which in turn fosters a closer relationship with Him. As believers experience the joy and fulfillment that comes from loving others, their faith is reinforced, and they become more committed to living out the Gospel in their daily lives.

2. Transformation of Relationships: Love as a witness has the power to transform relationships, both within the church and in the broader community. When believers commit to loving one another as Christ has loved them, their relationships become stronger, healthier, and more Christ-centered. This love fosters an environment of trust, unity, and mutual support, which not only benefits the individual relationships but also strengthens the overall witness of the church.

3. Evangelistic Impact: One of the most significant impacts of love as a witness is its evangelistic power. When non-believers see the love of Christ demonstrated in the lives of believers, they are more likely to be open to hearing

the message of the Gospel. Love has the power to break down barriers, heal wounds, and draw people to the truth of Christ. As believers live out their faith through love, they become effective witnesses for Christ, leading others to experience the transformative power of the Gospel.

4. Promotion of Unity and Reconciliation: Love as a witness promotes unity and reconciliation, both within the church and in the broader community. When believers commit to loving one another and seeking reconciliation, they create an environment of peace and harmony. This unity serves as a powerful testimony to the world of the reality of Christ and the power of the Gospel to bring people together. Additionally, love as a witness can help to heal divisions and promote reconciliation in the broader community, reflecting the inclusive and reconciling love of Christ.

5. Inspiration for Service and Generosity: Love as a witness inspires believers to serve and give generously of their time, resources, and talents. When believers see the impact of love in the lives of others, they are motivated to continue serving and giving in order to further the work of the Gospel. This service and generosity not only meet practical needs but also serve as a powerful testimony to the love of Christ.

6. Creation of a Legacy of Love: Love as a witness has the power to create a lasting legacy of love that extends beyond the individual believer and impacts future generations. When believers live out their faith through love, they create a ripple effect that influences their families, communities, and even the broader culture. This legacy of love serves as a powerful testimony to the enduring power of the Gospel and the reality of Christ's love.

Testimonies of Love as a Witness

Throughout history, there have been countless examples of how love has served as a powerful witness to the reality of Christ. These testimonies illustrate the impact of love as a witness and serve as an inspiration for believers to continue living out their faith through love. Here are a few examples:

1. Mother Teresa's Ministry of Love: Mother Teresa is one of the most well-known examples of love as a witness. Her ministry to the poor and dying in Calcutta, India, was motivated by her deep love for Christ and her desire to serve Him by loving the least of these. Through her selfless service and love,

Mother Teresa became a powerful witness to the love of Christ, drawing people from all walks of life to the Gospel. Her legacy of love continues to inspire millions of people around the world to live out their faith through acts of love and service.

2. Corrie ten Boom's Forgiveness: Corrie ten Boom, a Dutch Christian who helped to hide Jews during the Holocaust, is another example of love as a witness. After being imprisoned in a concentration camp and losing her sister, Corrie was faced with the challenge of forgiving those who had wronged her. With God's help, she was able to forgive, even when it seemed impossible. Her story of forgiveness and love became a powerful witness to the reality of Christ and the power of the Gospel to bring healing and reconciliation. Corrie's testimony continues to inspire believers to choose love and forgiveness, even in the face of great suffering.

3. Martin Luther King Jr.'s Advocacy for Justice: Martin Luther King Jr. is an example of how love can be a powerful witness in the pursuit of justice. As a leader of the civil rights movement in the United States, King advocated for racial equality and justice through nonviolent means, motivated by his Christian faith and love for all people. His commitment to love and nonviolence served as a powerful witness to the world, demonstrating the transformative power of the Gospel to bring about social change. King's legacy of love and justice continues to inspire believers to work for justice and equality in their own communities.

4. The Early Church's Witness of Love: As mentioned earlier, the early Christian church provides a powerful example of how love can serve as a witness to the world. The early believers' commitment to love, unity, and generosity set them apart from the rest of society and served as a powerful testimony to the reality of Christ. Their love for one another and for those in need drew people to the faith and contributed to the rapid spread of the Gospel throughout the Roman Empire. The early church's example continues to inspire believers to live out their faith through love, creating communities that reflect the love of Christ.

5. The Amish Community's Forgiveness: In 2006, a tragic school shooting took place in an Amish community in Pennsylvania, resulting in the deaths of five young girls. In the aftermath of the shooting, the Amish community's response of forgiveness and love became a powerful witness to the world.

Despite their grief and loss, the community chose to forgive the shooter and even reached out to his family with love and support. This act of forgiveness served as a testimony to the love of Christ and demonstrated the power of the Gospel to bring healing and reconciliation. The Amish community's response continues to inspire believers to choose love and forgiveness, even in the face of great tragedy.

Conclusion

Love is not only a commandment but also a powerful witness to the reality of Christ in the life of a believer. As Jesus taught in John 13:34-35, it is through love that the world will know that we are His disciples. This love is not just a sentiment or a feeling but a tangible expression of our faith that has the power to transform lives, heal relationships, and draw others to the truth of the Gospel.

In reflecting on the theological significance of love as a witness, we are reminded that love is the essence of the Christian life and the foundation upon which all other aspects of faith are built. Love is the evidence of our relationship with Christ and the means by which we participate in the ongoing revelation of God's love to the world.

As we seek to demonstrate love as a witness in our daily lives, may we be inspired by the examples of those who have gone before us, who have lived out their faith through acts of love, service, forgiveness, and generosity. Let us commit to loving one another as Christ has loved us, and to sharing that love with the world in practical and tangible ways.

In a world that is often marked by division, conflict, and self-interest, the witness of love stands as a beacon of hope and light. As we live out this love in our relationships, communities, and beyond, we participate in God's redemptive work, bringing the reality of Christ to a world in need of His love and grace. Let us strive to be faithful witnesses of Christ's love, that through our love, others may come to know and experience the transforming power of the Gospel.

Chapter 15: The Divine Heart of Love

Introduction

Love is the essence of the Christian faith and the heartbeat of God's relationship with humanity. Throughout this book, we have explored various dimensions of love—its eternal nature, its role as a witness, its power to heal and transform, and its expression through forgiveness, humility, and sacrifice. As we come to the concluding chapter, we are invited to reflect on the overarching theme that has woven these threads together: the divine heart of love. This chapter will focus on the centrality of God's love, as expressed in Psalm 136:26, "Give thanks to the God of heaven. His love endures forever." This verse encapsulates the inexhaustible and eternal nature of God's love—a love that not only sustains the universe but also reaches into the deepest corners of our lives and relationships.

In this chapter, we will delve into the theological significance of the divine heart of love, exploring how God's love is the source and model for all love. We will reflect on how this divine love is revealed in Scripture, particularly in the person of Jesus Christ, and how it is meant to flow into and through our own lives. Finally, we will offer practical guidance on how to seek and emulate this divine love in our relationships, encouraging readers to make God's heart of love the foundation of their lives.

The Theological Foundation of the Divine Heart of Love

The concept of God's love is not merely a theological idea but is central to the very nature and character of God. The Bible consistently affirms that God is love, and this love is the driving force behind His creation, redemption, and ongoing relationship with humanity. In 1 John 4:8, we read, "Whoever does not love does not know God, because God is love." This statement is profound because it does not simply say that God loves or that God has love; it says that God is love. Love is not just an attribute of God; it is His very essence. Everything that God does is motivated by and grounded in love.

Psalm 136, often referred to as the "Great Hallel," is a powerful reflection on the enduring love of God. Each verse in this psalm ends with the refrain, "His love endures forever," reminding us that God's love is unchanging, everlasting, and boundless. This psalm recounts the history of God's interactions with His people, highlighting His acts of creation, deliverance, provision, and protection. Throughout these verses, we see that God's love is not just a passive emotion but an active, dynamic force that accomplishes His purposes in the world. God's love is covenantal, meaning that it is rooted in His promises and His commitment to His people. It is a love that is faithful, even when we are faithless; a love that pursues, even when we wander; and a love that sacrifices, even to the point of death.

The divine heart of love is most fully revealed in the person of Jesus Christ. In John 3:16, we find the familiar and foundational declaration of God's love: "For God so loved the world that he gave his one and only Son, that whoever believes in him shall not perish but have eternal life." This verse encapsulates the gospel message, highlighting the sacrificial nature of God's love. Jesus is the embodiment of the divine heart of love—His life, death, and resurrection are the ultimate expression of God's love for humanity. Through Christ, we see that God's love is not distant or abstract but is deeply personal and transformative. It is a love that meets us where we are, redeems us from our sin, and invites us into a restored relationship with God.

The cross of Christ is the pinnacle of the divine heart of love. In Romans 5:8, Paul writes, "But God demonstrates his own love for us in this: While we were still sinners, Christ died for us." The cross reveals the depths of God's love—a love that is willing to suffer, to be humiliated, and to die for the sake of those He loves. It is a love that conquers sin and death, offering forgiveness, reconciliation, and new life. The resurrection of Christ further affirms the victory of this divine love, showing that love is stronger than death and that it has the power to bring about new creation.

In the person of the Holy Spirit, the divine heart of love continues to be poured out into our lives. In Romans 5:5, Paul writes, "And hope does not put us to shame, because God's love has been poured out into our hearts through the Holy Spirit, who has been given to us." The Holy Spirit is the presence of God's love within us, empowering us to love others as God has loved us. The Spirit transforms our hearts, enabling us to live out the divine love that we have received. It is through the Spirit that we are able to emulate the divine heart of love in our relationships, extending grace, mercy, and compassion to those around us.

Revealing the Divine Heart of Love in Scripture

The Bible is a love story—God's love story with humanity. From Genesis to Revelation, the narrative of Scripture is one of God's relentless pursuit of His people, motivated by His divine heart of love. This love is revealed in creation, in God's covenant with Israel, in the prophetic calls to repentance and restoration, and ultimately in the life, death, and resurrection of Jesus Christ.

1. Creation as an Act of Love: The story of God's love begins in the very act of creation. In Genesis 1, we read of God's creative work, as He brings the universe into existence with His word. Each act of creation is followed by the declaration that "it was good." Creation itself is an expression of God's love—a love that desires to create, to give life, and to establish a relationship with His creatures. Humanity, created in the image of God, is the pinnacle of this creation. In Genesis 2:7, we see the intimate nature of God's love as He forms Adam from the dust of the ground and breathes into his nostrils the breath of life. This act of creation is a reflection of the divine heart of love that seeks to give life and to be in communion with His creation.

2. Covenant as a Reflection of Divine Love: Throughout the Old Testament, God enters into covenants with His people, each one reflecting His unwavering love and commitment. The covenant with Noah after the flood, the covenant with Abraham promising descendants and land, and the covenant with Israel at Sinai are all expressions of God's love. These covenants reveal a God who is faithful, even when His people are not. In Deuteronomy 7:9, we read, "Know therefore that the Lord your God is God; he is the faithful God, keeping his covenant of love to a thousand generations of those who love him and keep his commandments." God's covenantal love is enduring and unbreakable, and it points forward to the new covenant established through Jesus Christ.

3. The Prophets and the Divine Heart of Love: The prophets of the Old Testament were messengers of God's love, calling His people to return to Him and to experience His grace and mercy. Despite the people's repeated unfaithfulness, God's love remained steadfast. In Hosea 11:1-4, we see a beautiful depiction of God's tender love for Israel: "When Israel was a child, I loved him, and out of Egypt I called my son. But the more they were called, the more they went away from me. They sacrificed to the Baals and they burned

incense to images. It was I who taught Ephraim to walk, taking them by the arms; but they did not realize it was I who healed them. I led them with cords of human kindness, with ties of love." This passage reveals the divine heart of love that longs for reconciliation and restoration, even in the face of rebellion.

4. Jesus Christ: The Embodiment of Divine Love: The ultimate revelation of the divine heart of love is found in Jesus Christ. In Him, the love of God takes on human form, entering into our world to bring salvation. Jesus' life was marked by love—He healed the sick, welcomed the outcast, forgave sinners, and taught about the kingdom of God. His love was radical and inclusive, breaking down barriers of race, gender, and social status. In John 15:13, Jesus declares, "Greater love has no one than this: to lay down one's life for one's friends." This love was most fully expressed on the cross, where Jesus willingly gave His life for the sake of humanity. The resurrection of Jesus is the ultimate triumph of love over sin and death, affirming that God's love is stronger than any force in the universe.

5. The Church as a Reflection of the Divine Heart of Love: The church, as the body of Christ, is called to be a reflection of the divine heart of love in the world. In Ephesians 5:1-2, Paul exhorts believers, "Follow God's example, therefore, as dearly loved children and walk in the way of love, just as Christ loved us and gave himself up for us as a fragrant offering and sacrifice to God." The church is to be a community marked by love—love for God, love for one another, and love for the world. This love is to be the defining characteristic of the church, serving as a witness to the reality of Christ and His kingdom.

6. The New Creation and the Fulfillment of Divine Love: The story of God's love culminates in the new creation, where the divine heart of love will be fully realized. In Revelation 21:1-4, we are given a vision of the new heaven and the new earth, where God will dwell with His people: "Then I saw 'a new heaven and a new earth,' for the first heaven and the first earth had passed away, and there was no longer any sea. I saw the Holy City, the new Jerusalem, coming down out of heaven from God, prepared as a bride beautifully dressed for her husband. And I heard a loud voice from the throne saying, 'Look! God's dwelling place is now among the people, and he will dwell with them. They will be his people, and God himself will be with them and be their God. He will wipe every tear from their eyes. There will be no more death or mourning or crying or pain, for the old order of things has passed away.'" In this new creation,

the divine heart of love will be fully experienced by all, as God's people are brought into perfect communion with Him for all eternity.

Seeking the Divine Heart of Love

The divine heart of love is not only something to be admired or studied; it is something to be sought after and emulated in our own lives. As believers, we are called to reflect the love of God in our relationships, allowing His love to flow through us and into the lives of others. Here are some practical ways to seek and emulate the divine heart of love:

1. Deepen Your Relationship with God: The foundation for emulating the divine heart of love is a deep and personal relationship with God. Spend time in prayer, worship, and the study of Scripture to grow in your knowledge of God's love and to experience His presence in your life. As you draw closer to God, His love will naturally overflow into your relationships with others. Seek to know God's heart and to align your own heart with His, allowing His love to shape your thoughts, attitudes, and actions.

2. Reflect on the Cross: The cross of Christ is the ultimate revelation of the divine heart of love. Take time to reflect on the significance of the cross and what it reveals about God's love for you. Consider the depth of God's love, as demonstrated through Jesus' willingness to suffer and die for your sake. Let this reflection inspire you to live a life of love and sacrifice, following in the footsteps of Christ. The more you meditate on the cross, the more you will be transformed by God's love and empowered to love others in the same way.

3. Embrace the Power of Forgiveness: Forgiveness is a powerful expression of the divine heart of love. Just as God has forgiven you through Christ, you are called to forgive others. Forgiveness is not always easy, but it is essential for maintaining healthy relationships and for reflecting God's love in your life. If there are unresolved conflicts or hurts in your relationships, take the initiative to seek reconciliation and to extend forgiveness. By doing so, you not only experience the freedom and healing that comes from forgiveness but also reflect the divine heart of love to others.

4. Practice Selflessness and Sacrifice: The divine heart of love is characterized by selflessness and sacrifice. In a world that often prioritizes self-interest and personal gain, choosing to put others' needs above your own

is a radical expression of God's love. Look for opportunities to serve others, whether in small acts of kindness or in more significant ways. Be willing to make sacrifices for the sake of others, just as Christ made the ultimate sacrifice for you. As you practice selflessness and sacrifice, you will find that your love for others deepens and becomes more Christ-like.

5. Cultivate a Heart of Compassion: Compassion is at the core of the divine heart of love. Throughout His ministry, Jesus was moved with compassion for those who were hurting, marginalized, or in need. As His followers, we are called to cultivate the same heart of compassion. Look for opportunities to reach out to those who are suffering, to offer comfort and support, and to advocate for justice and mercy. Compassionate love reflects the divine heart of love and has the power to bring healing and transformation to the lives of others.

6. Commit to Humility and Service: Humility is essential for emulating the divine heart of love. Jesus, though He was in the form of God, humbled Himself and took on the form of a servant (Philippians 2:5-8). In the same way, we are called to humble ourselves and to serve others with a heart of love. Look for ways to serve those around you, whether in your family, church, or community. Be willing to take on tasks that may go unnoticed or unappreciated, knowing that your service is a reflection of the divine heart of love.

7. Pursue Unity and Reconciliation: The divine heart of love seeks to bring about unity and reconciliation in relationships. As followers of Christ, we are called to be peacemakers, working to heal divisions and to build bridges of understanding and trust. If there are areas of conflict or division in your life, take steps to pursue reconciliation. This may involve difficult conversations, the willingness to listen and understand, and the commitment to seek common ground. By pursuing unity and reconciliation, you reflect the divine heart of love and contribute to the healing of relationships.

8. Live with an Eternal Perspective: The divine heart of love is eternal, and it calls us to live with an eternal perspective. In a world that often focuses on the temporary and the immediate, choose to prioritize what will last into eternity—love, faith, and the relationships that are built on these foundations. Make decisions that reflect your commitment to God's eternal purposes, and invest in relationships that will have an eternal impact. By living with an eternal

perspective, you align your heart with the divine heart of love and prepare yourself for the life to come.

9. Pray for the Holy Spirit's Guidance: The Holy Spirit is the presence of God's love within us, and He empowers us to live out the divine heart of love in our lives. Regularly pray for the Holy Spirit's guidance, asking Him to fill you with God's love and to help you reflect that love in your relationships. The Spirit will give you the wisdom, strength, and compassion you need to love others as God has loved you. Trust in the Spirit's work in your life, and be open to His leading as you seek to emulate the divine heart of love.

10. Express Gratitude for God's Love: Finally, cultivate a heart of gratitude for the divine heart of love that has been extended to you. Regularly thank God for His love, for the ways in which He has blessed you, and for the relationships He has placed in your life. Gratitude not only deepens your appreciation for God's love but also encourages you to share that love with others. As you express gratitude, you will find that your heart becomes more aligned with the divine heart of love, and you will be more motivated to live out that love in your daily life.

The Impact of Emulating the Divine Heart of Love

When we seek to emulate the divine heart of love in our lives, the impact is profound and far-reaching. This love not only transforms our own hearts but also has the power to change the lives of those around us. Here are some of the ways in which emulating the divine heart of love can impact your life and the lives of others:

1. Personal Transformation: Emulating the divine heart of love leads to personal transformation, as you become more like Christ in your character and conduct. As you grow in your understanding of God's love and allow that love to shape your life, you will experience a deepening of your relationship with God and a greater sense of purpose and fulfillment. This transformation will also be evident in your relationships, as you become more patient, forgiving, compassionate, and selfless.

2. Strengthened Relationships: The divine heart of love is the foundation for healthy, strong, and enduring relationships. When you reflect God's love in your interactions with others, your relationships become more resilient and

life-giving. Love fosters trust, unity, and mutual support, creating an environment where relationships can thrive. As you seek to emulate the divine heart of love, you will find that your relationships are strengthened and deepened, and that they become a source of joy and fulfillment.

3. Healing and Reconciliation: The divine heart of love has the power to bring healing and reconciliation to broken relationships. When you extend forgiveness, compassion, and grace to others, you open the door for healing and restoration. This love can heal wounds, mend divisions, and bring about reconciliation in even the most difficult situations. By emulating the divine heart of love, you become an instrument of God's healing in the lives of others.

4. A Witness to the World: Emulating the divine heart of love is a powerful witness to the world of the reality of Christ. In a world that is often marked by division, conflict, and self-interest, love stands out as a testimony to the transforming power of the Gospel. When others see the love of Christ reflected in your life, they are more likely to be drawn to the message of the Gospel and to experience the love of God for themselves. Your life becomes a living testimony to the divine heart of love, drawing others to Christ.

5. A Legacy of Love: Emulating the divine heart of love creates a lasting legacy of love that extends beyond your own life and impacts future generations. The love you show to others, the relationships you build, and the impact you have on the lives of those around you will continue to bear fruit long after you are gone. This legacy of love is a reflection of God's eternal love and serves as a powerful testimony to the enduring power of the Gospel.

6. Preparation for Eternity: Finally, emulating the divine heart of love prepares you for eternity. The love that you cultivate in this life is a foretaste of the love you will experience in the presence of God for all eternity. By aligning your heart with the divine heart of love, you are storing up treasures in heaven and participating in God's eternal kingdom. This love not only brings joy and fulfillment in this life but also prepares you for the life to come.

Conclusion

As we conclude this exploration of love, we are reminded that at the heart of it all is the divine heart of love—God's inexhaustible, eternal, and boundless love for His creation. This love is the foundation of our faith, the source of our relationships, and the ultimate goal of our lives. It is a love that has been revealed in creation, in covenant, in the cross of Christ, and in the outpouring of the Holy Spirit. It is a love that we are called to seek, to emulate, and to share with others.

Psalm 136:26 invites us to "Give thanks to the God of heaven. His love endures forever." This enduring love is not just something to be admired from a distance; it is something to be experienced, embraced, and lived out in our daily lives. As we seek to emulate the divine heart of love, we are participating in God's redemptive work, bringing His love into a world that is in desperate need of it.

In a world that is often marked by division, conflict, and self-interest, the divine heart of love stands as a beacon of hope and light. As we live out this love in our relationships, communities, and beyond, we reflect the character of God and draw others to the reality of His love. Let us commit to seeking and emulating the divine heart of love, that our lives may be a reflection of God's enduring love and a testimony to the power of the Gospel.

May the divine heart of love guide you, inspire you, and fill you, as you seek to live a life that honors God and blesses others. And may you experience the fullness of God's love in your own life, as you reflect that love to a world in need.

Don't miss out!

Visit the website below and you can sign up to receive emails whenever Michelle Renee Thomas publishes a new book. There's no charge and no obligation.

https://books2read.com/r/B-A-CIRYB-AYLIF

BOOKS 2 READ

Connecting independent readers to independent writers.

About the Author

Michelle Renee Thomas is an acclaimed author of Christian fiction, known for her inspiring novels that explore faith, hope, and redemption. With a background in theology, Michelle crafts stories that reflect the transformative power of God's love and the resilience of the human spirit. Her rich characters and profound spiritual insights offer solace and encouragement. Living in the countryside with her family, Michelle draws inspiration from nature and her faith community. Her books have touched many hearts, making her a beloved voice in faith-based literature.